D1594529

by the same author

BRIDGE: MODERN BIDDING
BRIDGE IN THE MENAGERIE
BRIDGE IN THE FOURTH DIMENSION
INSTANT BRIDGE
BRIDGE UNLIMITED
BRIDGE COURSE COMPLETE
THE FINER ARTS OF BRIDGE
STREAMLINE YOUR BIDDING

in collaboration with Nico Gardener
CARD PLAY TECHNIQUE

in collaboration with Eric Jannersten
THE BEST OF BRIDGE

in collaboration with Aksel J. Nielsen
DEFENCE AT BRIDGE

Pocket Guides
WINNING BIDDING
WINNING DEFENCE
WINNING CONVENTIONS

Pocket Guide Distributors
L.S.P. Books
8 Farncombe Street, Godalming, Surrey

Bridge
Case for the Defence

BRIDGE
Case for the Defence

VICTOR MOLLO

FABER AND FABER
London & Boston

First published in 1970
by Faber and Faber Limited
3 Queen Square London WC1
Reprinted 1972
First published in Faber Paperbacks 1979
Printed in Great Britain by
Lowe & Brydone Printers Limited
Thetford Norfolk
All rights reserved

British Library Cataloguing in Publication Data

Mollo, Victor
  Bridge, case for the defence.
  1. Contract bridge
  I. Title
  795.4′153   GV1282.3
  ISBN 0–571–11440–7

Acknowledgements

I am innocent on all counts. The guilty parties are, of course, Nico Gardener and my wife, the Squirrel.

Nico is unlike any other computer. You do not have to feed him with the right information to get the correct answer. For that matter, if I had the right information, would I feed him at all? Nico's principal merit is that he gives me the right answer when I give him the wrong information, so I know that if a hand gets past him, no one else in this incarnation is likely to pull me up.

Technical infallibility in a partner at the table is a serious liability for it takes so long to prove him wrong. In a bridge writer's guru it is a considerable asset, and providing that Nico stays that way, I shall continue to overlook his other blemishes. After all, no one can be infallible without having grave faults to make up for it.

Indulgence, however, need not be carried too far and should you find that I have slipped up anywhere, please do not hesitate to complain—to Nico.

I turn to the other guilty party—my wife. She watches everything I do and doesn't trust me an inch. More especially, she suspects me of not caring how many players are allotted the same card on the same deal. Are North and West both harbouring the ◇ 5? Hasn't anyone the ♣ 3? Is it fair that East should have no more than twelve cards? My wife, who types everything I write, reproaches me with callous indifference. And she is not prepared to overlook the slightest peccadillo, no matter how little bearing it may have on my noble theme. I humour her, naturally, and adjust every suit and every hand to meet her demands. But there can be no power without responsibility and should you detect any card out of place in the 8,000 or more in this book, place the blame

7

ACKNOWLEDGEMENTS

fairly and squarely on the frailties of the wife, not on the venial lapses of the erring husband.

I have one more debt to acknowledge. I am under the deepest obligation to all those Souths who have, for years, brought home against me contracts which I should have broken. It has been worth every penny and every matchpoint for, by losing, I learned to win and can now pass on the know-how to my readers.

Contents

Acknowledgements   *page* 7
Author's Preface   11

PART ONE

Curtain Raiser   17
Quizzes 1–6   18
Dummy Goes Down   24
Quizzes 7–50   26

PART TWO

Greek Chorus   117
Quizzes 51–100   118

PART THREE

A Foreword   217
Quizzes 101–150   218

Author's Preface

The difference between the best players and the small minority who are not, can usually be measured by a stop-watch. The former do the right thing. The latter would also do it if they knew what it was—in time. The purpose of this book is to bridge the gap between the two, which is often no more than a few seconds.

Beginners apart, most of the mistakes at the bridge table are made, not because players do not know what to do, but because they don't know when to do it.

They learned long ago how to force declarer, and more recently how not to force him, when he had to reduce his trumps. But when was that? How soon could one guess his intentions?

To husband high cards jealously is second nature to a player of experience. Yet he knows that, on occasion, when declarer plans to throw him in, he must get rid of his aces and kings, and retain deuces and threes as exit cards. But when exactly is the time to do it? What are the first signs and symptoms that an end-play is afoot?

In the days of my bridge adolescence, I devoured textbook after textbook. When I knew everything, I set out to learn the rest—the part that really mattered—at the bridge table. For I soon realized that bridge is like an iceberg. Technique is the top which shows above the surface. The greater part, born of judgement and experience, is submerged below.

Hence the form of this book. Quiz book and textbook in one, it seeks to reproduce as nearly as possible the conditions at the card table. Every hand presents a problem, often a simple one, but until the player has identified it, he is groping in the dark and unlikely, therefore, to find the solution.

So the emphasis in these pages is always on IDENTIFICATION.

AUTHOR'S PREFACE

The quiz comes first, then the answer, and finally the post-mortem. The logic of the sequence is obvious, yet by the nature of things the orthodox textbook is rarely able to follow it. For one thing, chapter headings give away the subject and, as each theme is developed in orderly fashion, the reader knows what's coming, and therefore, what is expected of him. It is, alas, unavoidable, but all too often the cure precedes the diagnosis and the inquest comes before the corpse.

Here the reader must fend for himself and discover later where he went wrong. And to help him resist the temptation of making 'later' come too soon, the answer to every quiz is given overleaf, easy to get at, yet not too easy to peep at.

SHAPE OF THINGS TO COME

In conception and design this book follows closely its predecessor on dummy play, *Victor Mollo's Winning Double*.* Carefully planned disorder is a feature of the pattern, so should the reader detect any flaw in the disarrangement, I crave his indulgence. It is not intentional, except once or twice in Part One, which differs basically from Parts Two and Three.

The first fifty quizzes present the reader with the rich armoury available to the defence, and it may require, on occasion, two consecutive examples to illustrate the use of a particular weapon. In quizzes 51 to 150, IDENTIFICATION and RECOGNITION reign supreme. The situations are the same as before, but most of them are more difficult and there is no revealing juxtaposition to indicate the nature of the problem.

The reader is expected to make numerous mistakes and grievous ones at that. If he doesn't, I shall have failed in my purpose, for he cannot learn from questions to which he knows the answers already. Conversely, the more he errs, the more will he gain, for with every lapse he will acquire something he did not have before —the knowhow to avoid it in future.

Just as the expert will find some of the first fifty quizzes too easy, so others may find a few of those that follow too difficult.

* The title of the American edition is *How Good is Your Bridge?* (Harold H. Hart, New York).

AUTHOR'S PREFACE

But then, in real life, too, very difficult hands come up from time to time, so it would be unrealistic to avoid them altogether. They will not occur too often and I promise that, unlike the scientist who invented a cure for which there is no known disease, I shall indulge in no acrobatics designed solely to dazzle and bemuse. If, on occasion, a spectacular play is called for, it is of a type which happens more often than is generally realized and with which a good player should, therefore, be familiar.

A PROPHESY—AND A CHALLENGE

I predict with confidence that by the time the reader has reached the last of the quizzes, his defence will have improved considerably, and what is more, he will be able to measure the improvement himself.

As in my Quiz-Textbook on dummy play, marks are awarded for the last hundred quizzes. For the most part, the correct answers earn five marks each, but at times, the bonus rises to 8 and to 10.

With malice aforethought, I have introduced an artificial partition between Parts Two and Three. This is to provide a basis of comparison, so that the sceptical student should have tangible proof that as he reads on, he is making real and appreciable progress.

The total, unattainable, I hope, is the same for Part Two and Part Three. Each group of fifty quizzes earns 350 marks, but I defy the reader not to return a higher score for the last group of fifty than for the one before.

Is there a trap? Is Part Three easier by any chance than Part Two? That would be a simple way for the author to score a meretricious success. Fortunately, it is simpler still for the reader to catch him out and establish beyond doubt whether or not his progress is genuine. All he need do, if he is so minded, is to tackle Part Three before Part Two. There is no difference in kind between the two groups of quizzes, but should he reverse the natural order, the reader will reach a higher total for the second group than for the third.

This is a challenge. I believe that the Quiz-Textbook approach is the best and simplest method of imparting the art of good bridge. So I shall close this preface by echoing the earnest plea of the inventor to the airman taking off to test a new type of parachute: 'Do your best. Your success will mean a lot to me.'

Part One

Curtain Raiser

Many more errors are committed by West than by East, for his is the post of honour. He fires the first shot, and if he mistakes the target, he can lose the battle before it is joined in earnest.

There are rules and tables in plenty to help West in his hour of need. By leading the fourth highest of his longest suit or the top of a sequence or the lowest from three to an honour, he will not always strike the best opening, but he will usually avoid the worst one. The guiding principles, passed on to us by our forefathers from the days of whist, are sound in themselves and have much to commend them.

The expert, however, often does better. Looking beyond ancient clichés—and modern ones, too, for that matter—he knows how to listen. Tuning in and drawing inferences from every bid and every pass, he seeks to wrench from opponents themselves the key to their undoing.

Does it look as if they are playing with a 4–3 trump fit? That is the time to force them. Will declarer find ruffing value in dummy? West can reduce it by opening a trump. If the contract sounds shaky, he looks for a passive lead, intent on giving nothing away. Conversely, when it is clear from the start that the defence will be heavily outgunned, he does not hesitate to take risks, to gamble on finding his partner with this or that singleton, this or that honour card, even if by so doing he may give away an extra trick.

Before dummy goes down in each one of the three parts of this book, the reader is introduced to six quizzes on opening leads. To select the right one he should listen carefully to everything North–South say—and don't say—allowing no sound to escape him. For though the opening lead is proverbially blind, it should never be deaf.

QUESTIONS

(1)

South bids 1 NT (16–18) which North raises to 3 NT. What should West lead from:

(a) ♠ K J 10 9 6
   ♡ Q 4 2
   ◇ J 7 4
   ♣ K 6

(b) ♠ K J 10 9 6 4 3
   ♡ 5 2
   ◇ 7 4
   ♣ K 6

(2)

(a) ♠ K J 10 9 6
   ♡ 4
   ◇ Q J 10 8 3
   ♣ K 6

(b) ♠ J 10
   ♡ 8 7 6 5 4 3 2
   ◇ J 10
   ♣ J 10

QUESTIONS

(3)

(a) ♠ A 2
    ♡ 8 7 6 5 4 3
    ◇ A 7
    ♣ K J 10

(b) ♠ A Q 10 2
    ♡ A J 9 4
    ◇ K Q 5
    ♣ 5 3

(4)

NORTH DEALS.

South	North
—	Pass
1 ♠	3 ♠
Pass	—

What should West lead from:

(a) ♠ J 10 2
    ♡ A 10 4
    ◇ K Q 9
    ♣ Q 7 6 3

(b) ♠ J 4 3
    ♡ K 2
    ◇ 7 5 4 2
    ♣ 8 6 5 2

(c) ♠ J 10 2
    ♡ 2
    ◇ Q 10 7 5
    ♣ K 9 4 3 2

(d) ♠ J 10 9 6
    ♡ 2
    ◇ K 10 7 5
    ♣ K 9 4 3

ANSWERS

(1)

(*a*) ♠ J.

This holding is known as an 'interior sequence'. The lead of the jack may help to catch the queen, especially if partner has A x (x) and South holds the queen.

Similarly, from A J 10 x x, the correct lead is the J, but. . . .

(*b*) ♠ K.

The ♠ J will still be much the best lead if partner has A x and declarer Q x x, but it's asking too much to expect this particular distribution. A better chance with so long a suit is to find a singleton queen in dummy. Note that if partner has the bare queen the suit will be blocked—unless West opens the king.

(2)

(*a*) ◇ Q.

There is as good a chance of finding partner with an honour in diamonds as in spades, but whereas a spade opening can cost a trick, a diamond lead is safe. Moreover, the ♠ K may eventually provide an entry to the diamonds, which is more than the diamonds are ever likely to do for the spades.

(*b*) ♠ J.

There is no hope whatever of bringing in the hearts. Even if partner produces the A K—or the A K Q for that matter— West has no entry.

The spade jack is slightly better than the other two. More no-trump contracts are played with a long minor than with a long major, so if there's a five or six card spade suit about, partner is more likely to have it than declarer or his dummy.

ANSWERS

(3)

(*a*) A heart.

With entries in three suits, West has distinct hopes of setting up tricks in hearts. No one could seriously object to the lead of the ♡ 8, the top of a sequence, or to the ♡ 5, the four highest, but this isn't a case for the 'correct' lead. Partner is likely to play a secondary role and a deceptive card—the ♡ 3, perhaps —couldn't be crimed.

(*b*) ♣ 5.

Partner can hardly have a single point, so West's sole concern should be to give nothing away and wait patiently for the tricks to come to him.

(4)

(*a*) ♠ 2.

The bidding suggests ruffing value and West's first concern should be to reduce it. When responder supports opener's suit, a trump lead is often the best.

Should East have an honour in trumps, the lead of the jack or ten may cost a trick, and whatever the distribution, it can hardly gain.

(*b*) ♡ K.

On the bidding East is marked with a good deal of strength. Why else have North-South stopped short of game? West can hope, therefore, to find partner with the ♡ A or maybe with the ♡ Q and a quick entry in trumps. In either event he will get a heart ruff, perhaps two ruffs.

(*c*) ♡ 2.

A singleton is a routine lead against a suit contract. West hopes for a ruff, but. . . .

(*d*) The ♠ J.

With four trumps, West is in no hurry to ruff. On the contrary, he is more concerned with stopping ruffs by declarer.

QUESTIONS

(5)

SOUTH DEALS.

South	West	North	East
1 ♠	Pass	2 ◇	Pass
2 NT	Pass	3 NT	Dble

What should West lead from:

(a) ♠ Q 7 6 4 2 (b) ♠ A Q 4
    ♡ Q 10 3 2   ♡ 7 6 2
    ◇ J   ◇ J
    ♣ K 3 2   ♣ Q J 10 9 8 7

(6)

SOUTH DEALS.

South	West	North	East
1 ♠	Pass	3 ◇	Pass
4 ◇	Pass	4 ♠	Pass
6 ♠	Pass	Pass	Dble

What should West lead from:

(a) ♠ 7 6 5 (b) ♠ 7 6 5
    ♡ K Q J   ♡ 8 2
    ◇ J 5 3 2   ◇ A J 6 2
    ♣ Q 4 2   ♣ A K 6 2

ANSWERS

(5)

(*a*) ◇ J.

There can be no doubt that East doubled for a diamond lead. It is the accepted meaning of a double in that position and West's singleton fits into the picture. Clearly, East has good diamonds over North, who bid the suit. Glad to oblige, West leads his ◇ J, but. . . .

(*b*) ♣ Q.

The inferences are the same as before, but this time West has a good suit of his own and two probable entries. Partner doesn't know it and his double should be treated as a request, not as a command.

In this situation, as in every other, a player's first duty to his partner is to use his own judgement.

(6)

(*a*) and (*b*)

A diamond.

East's is unmistakably a Lightner Double, calling for an *unusual* lead. There would be nothing unusual about leading an unbid suit or a trump. The bidding and West's length in diamonds indicate that East has a void and will ruff the opening diamond lead.

In (*b*) declarer or his dummy is surely void of clubs.

The Lightner Double* applies only to slam contracts, but is then often invaluable.

* Named after Theodore Lightner, a member of Ely Culbertson's all-conquering team in the early years of Contract Bridge.

Dummy Goes Down

West has led, and as dummy goes down, East joins the fray. Declarer's line of play will soon reveal his intentions, his hopes, his fears, his expectations. But what is his distribution? What exactly is his high card strength?

As before, the bidding remains the best source of information, especially in the early stages. A pass can be as eloquent as a bid, but where the auction is uncontested the reader will find only the North–South sequence given in full. This is not, as he doubtless suspects, because the author was too lazy to fill in every pass by East and West. There is an even better reason. At the card table defenders must remember what happened and may not ask for a review of the bidding after the opening lead has been made. It should, therefore, be the same here. Like the dog which did not bark in the night, the words 'E/W pass throughout' tell their story. The reader is entitled to no other reminder.

Vulnerability does not fall into quite the same category. It is significant part of the time, but to give it only when it matters would be, again, an artificial aid to the reader which he will not find in the cold, bleak world outside. And so, unlike the East–West passes, the state of vulnerability is announced on every deal.

With a few clearly noted exceptions, all the hands which follow occur at rubber bridge or in teams of four matches, not in pairs events where the method of scoring introduces special problems.

No reader on either side of the Atlantic need worry about systems. The bidding is always natural, fitting Acol or Standard American equally well, with Blackwood and Stayman as the only conventions in general use.

The opening 1 notrump varies according to vulnerability, but for this there is a special reason unconnected with the merits of

24

DUMMY GOES DOWN

Acol, Kaplan-Sheinwold or any other system, British or American.

Often the most difficult and always the most important task of the defender is to form quickly an accurate picture of declarer's hand. The best guide, as has been noted already, is the bidding, and no bid carries more inferences than 1 notrump, revealing in one breath both shape and strength. Since hands in the 12–14 group occur far more frequently than those ranging from 16–18, the weak notrump provides the reader with much useful practice in card-reading.

Most of the time, the notrump range is given after the bid as a reminder to the reader, but throughout these pages it conforms to the same standard—16–18 vulnerable, 12–14 non-vulnerable.

Finally, from A K we shall lead the king. The lead of the ace, for which there is much to be said, is gaining in popularity among European tournament players, but by and large, the traditional lead of the king still has most followers. So we will join the majority.

And now the reader knows everything. As West, he should break some of the contracts all the time. As East, he should break all the contracts some of the time. And if he does his stuff in both positions, South will assuredly lose all his contracts all the time.

(7)

♠ A K
♡ Q J 10 9 7
◇ K Q 10
♣ A 10 2

```
        N
    W       E
        S
```

♠ 7 6
♡ K 8 3
◇ J 9 7 6
♣ J 9 6 5

Neither side vulnerable
Dealer: South

South	*North*
Pass	1 ♡
1 NT	3 NT

E/W pass throughout

CONTRACT: 3 NT.

West leads, the ♠ Q to dummy's ♠ K.
Declarer plays the ♡ Q.
What card should East play?

(8)

♠ A
♡ A K 10 8 7
◇ 8 5
♣ A J 9 8 2

```
      N
   W     E
      S
```

♠ 7 6
♡ J 9 5 3
◇ K 9 7
♣ Q 10 7 6

Neither side vulnerable
Dealer: South

South	North
Pass	1 ♡
2 ◇	3 ♣
3 NT	

E/W pass throughout

CONTRACT: 3 NT.

West leads the ♠ Q to dummy's ace.
Declarer calls for the ◇ 8.
Which card should East play?

ANSWERS

♡ K.

This has nothing to do with the 'cover an honour with an honour' adage. The purpose in covering honours is to promote lesser cards and here all the lesser cards, down to the seven, are on view, so there can be nothing to promote.

The focus is on partner's spades, not on dummy's hearts. West can have one ace, but not two. South did bid 1 NT, after all. If West has the ◇ A or no ace at all, the contract is unbreakable. If he has the ♡ A, it is unmakeable—providing East goes up with his ♡ K at trick two, while he has a spade to play.

(8)

$\Diamond$ K.

Basically, the position is the same as in the previous example. There is little prospect of defeating the contract without bringing in partner's spades and the only possible entry partner can have is the $\Diamond$ A. If he hasn't got it, all is lost anyway. If he has it, that vital entry must be preserved at all cost, until the ♠ K has been driven out.

Observe what happens if East does *not* go up with his $\Diamond$ K. West wins with the $\Diamond$ A, leads a spade, drives out the king and sets up his suit. East comes in with the $\Diamond$ K and has no spade left to play.

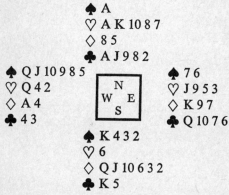

QUESTIONS

(9)

♠ A 4
♡ Q 10 7
◇ 5 3
♣ A J 10 6 5 3

(a) ♠ K Q 10 8
♡ 9 8 5 2
◇ 10 7 6
♣ K 7

```
    N
  W   E
    S
```

(b) ♠ K Q 10 8
♡ 9 8 5
◇ 10 7 6
♣ K Q 7

Neither side vulnerable
Dealer: North

South	North
—	1 ♣
1 ◇	2 ♣
3 NT	

E/W pass throughout

CONTRACT: 3 NT.

West leads the ♠ K, which holds, then the ♠ 8 to dummy's ace. Declarer crosses to his hand with a diamond to the king and leads the ♣ 8.

Which card should West play?

QUESTIONS

(10)

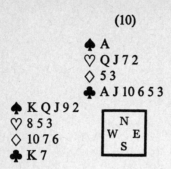

♠ A
♡ Q J 7 2
◇ 5 3
♣ A J 10 6 5 3

♠ K Q J 9 2
♡ 8 5 3
◇ 10 7 6
♣ K 7

Neither side vulnerable
Dealer: North

South	West	North	East
—	—	1 ♣	Pass
1 ◇	Pass	2 ♣	Pass
3 NT			

CONTRACT: 3 NT.

West leads the ♠ K to dummy's ♠ A.
Declarer crosses to his hand with a diamond to the king and leads the ♣ 9.
Which card should West play?

ANSWERS

(9)

(*a*) ♣ K.

To sever communications between the closed hand and dummy. If declarer goes up with the ♣ A, he will have no entry to the table. If he ducks, and finesses next time, playing West for the K Q x, he will not make a club at all—unless he has three clubs himself.

(*b*) ♣ 7.

This keeps declarer to two club tricks—unless he has three himself.

ANSWERS

(10)

Yes, this looks very much like the last example, but appearances are deceptive. West has one more spade than before and he doesn't mind declarer scoring five tricks in clubs, so long as he wins four tricks in spades first—and beats the contract.

Declarer doesn't know how many spades West has and if, as his play indicates, he is seeking to develop the club suit, he will duck on the first round. Should West go up with the ♣ K to disrupt communications—the correct play in the previous example—declarer may be driven, in sheer desperation, to make his contract. He will need the heart finesse, then the diamond finesse and a 3–3 diamond break—and all will come off as in this diagram.

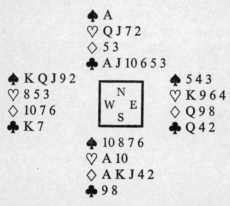

The moral is: *every* case should be treated on its merits—including the case for severing declarer's communications with dummy.

QUESTIONS

(11)

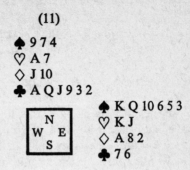

♠ 9 7 4
♡ A 7
◇ J 10
♣ A Q J 9 3 2

```
        N
    W       E
        S
```

♠ K Q 10 6 5 3
♡ K J
◇ A 8 2
♣ 7 6

Neither side vulnerable
Dealer: South

South	West	North	East
Pass	Pass	1 ♣	1 ♠
2 NT	Pass	3 NT	—

CONTRACT: 3 NT.

West leads the ♠ 8 to East's queen and South's ace.
Declarer plays a club to dummy's queen and continues with the
◇ J.
Which card should East play?

QUESTIONS

(12)

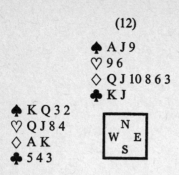

♠ A J 9
♡ 9 6
♢ Q J 10 8 6 3
♣ K J

♠ K Q 3 2
♡ Q J 8 4
♢ A K
♣ 5 4 3

N
W E
S

E/W vulnerable
Dealer: North

South	West	North	East
—	—	1 ♢	Pass
2 ♣	Pass	2 ♢	Pass
3 NT			

CONTRACT: 3 NT.

West leads the ♡ 4.
Declarer wins with the ♡ 10, and plays a diamond to West's king.
What should West lead at trick three?

(11)

◇ A.

. . . firmly, then, no less firmly, the ♠ K. As always, East should count declarer's tricks. In addition to the ♠ A, he can see six clubs and the ♡ A. If South started with ♠ A J 2, there is no hope. But maybe West has the missing ♠ 2. If so, the jack will fall on the king and the contract will go two down.

Why, then, does declarer risk leading the ◇ J? To steal his ninth trick quickly, which he will succeed in doing if East is not on the alert.

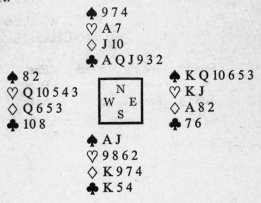

```
                    ♠ 9 7 4
                    ♡ A 7
                    ◇ J 10
                    ♣ A Q J 9 3 2
    ♠ 8 2              N          ♠ K Q 10 6 5 3
    ♡ Q 10 5 4 3    W     E       ♡ K J
    ◇ Q 6 5 3          S          ◇ A 8 2
    ♣ 10 8                        ♣ 7 6
                    ♠ A J
                    ♡ 9 8 6 2
                    ◇ K 9 7 4
                    ♣ K 5 4
```

(12)

♠ 2.

South's 3 NT bid shows at least 13 points. West has 15 and can see 12 in dummy, leaving none for East. Yet despite his powerful hand, West cannot beat the contract on his own. What can East do to help? There is just one precious card he may have—the ♠ 10. And if so, the day may yet be saved.

On West's ♠ 2 declarer, not knowing the position, will doubtless play dummy's nine. Winning with the ♠ 10, a surprised East will return a spade and the defence will take three spades to beat the contract.

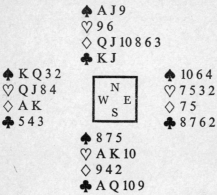

```
              ♠ A J 9
              ♡ 9 6
              ◇ Q J 10 8 6 3
              ♣ K J

  ♠ K Q 3 2         N          ♠ 10 6 4
  ♡ Q J 8 4      W     E       ♡ 7 5 3 2
  ◇ A K            S           ◇ 7 5
  ♣ 5 4 3                      ♣ 8 7 6 2

              ♠ 8 7 5
              ♡ A K 10
              ◇ 9 4 2
              ♣ A Q 10 9
```

The moral is: if, to beat the contract, partner must have a particular card, assume that he has it. It is surprising how often the best defence ties in WISHFUL THINKING.

(13)

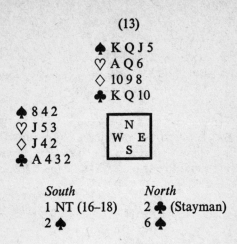

♠ K Q J 5
♡ A Q 6
◇ 10 9 8
♣ K Q 10

♠ 8 4 2
♡ J 5 3
◇ J 4 2
♣ A 4 3 2

South	*North*
1 NT (16–18)	2 ♣ (Stayman)
2 ♠	6 ♠

N/S vulnerable
Dealer: South
E/W pass throughout

CONTRACT: 6 ♠.

West led the ♠ 4.

Declarer drew trumps, East following twice, and went one down.

Which two tricks did he lose and in which order did he lose them?

QUESTIONS

(14)

♠ K 10 8
♡ 8
◇ Q 7 5
♣ K J 7 6 3 2

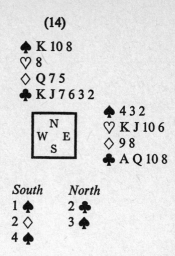

♠ 4 3 2
♡ K J 10 6
◇ 9 8
♣ A Q 10 8

South	North
1 ♠	2 ♣
2 ◇	3 ♠
4 ♠	

E/W vulnerable
Dealer: South
E/W pass throughout

CONTRACT: 4 ♠.

West leads the ♠ A, then the ♠ 6.
Declarer wins in dummy and leads the ♡ 8.
Which card should East play?

ANSWERS

(13)

♣ J, then the ♣ A.

West can see 23 points—6 in his own hand and 17 in dummy. Since South's vulnerable 1 NT promises 16–18, East can have at most one jack—to be precise, the ♣ J for the three others are on view. What's more, East *must* have that jack. Otherwise declarer would have tabled his hand, conceding a trick to the ♣ A.

Realizing declarer's problem, West prepares *mentally* to play low when a club is led towards dummy. Declarer will doubtless go up with the ♣ K, return to his hand and lead another club.

Again West must play low without batting an eyelid. Let declarer bat—and misguess, which he will do part of the time.

It doesn't require great skill to play low twice in clubs, but only a good player, having worked out the hand in advance, will do so with effortless ease—and it's no use doing it otherwise.

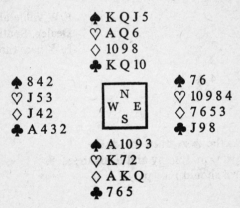

```
              ♠ K Q J 5
              ♡ A Q 6
              ◇ 10 9 8
              ♣ K Q 10
  ♠ 8 4 2         N          ♠ 7 6
  ♡ J 5 3    W         E     ♡ 10 9 8 4
  ◇ J 4 2         S          ◇ 7 6 5 3
  ♣ A 4 3 2                  ♣ J 9 8
              ♠ A 10 9 3
              ♡ K 7 2
              ◇ A K Q
              ♣ 7 6 5
```

ANSWERS

(14)

♡ K.

East wants to be on play since he has a trump to lead and West probably hasn't.

Going up with the ♡ K cannot cost a trick even if declarer has the ♡ A Q. Should he need the finesse he will take it anyway.

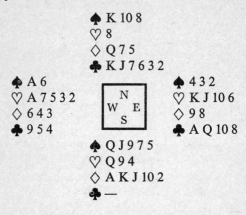

```
                    ♠ K 10 8
                    ♡ 8
                    ◇ Q 7 5
                    ♣ K J 7 6 3 2
  ♠ A 6                              ♠ 4 3 2
  ♡ A 7 5 3 2        N               ♡ K J 10 6
  ◇ 6 4 3         W     E            ◇ 9 8
  ♣ 9 5 4            S               ♣ A Q 10 8
                    ♠ Q J 9 7 5
                    ♡ Q 9 4
                    ◇ A K J 10 2
                    ♣ —
```

QUESTIONS

(15)

♠ A K J 10
♡ 5 3
◇ A K 2
♣ A Q J 2

♠ Q 8 4 3
♡ J 2
◇ Q J 10 3
♣ 8 5 3

Neither side vulnerable
Dealer: West

South	West	North	East
—	Pass	1 ♣	Pass
Pass	2 ♡	Dble	Pass
2 ♠	Pass	4 ♠	

CONTRACT: 4 ♠.

West led the three top hearts.

Declarer, who followed all the way, ruffed the third heart in dummy with the ♠ 10 and the contract went one down.

(a) Which tricks did defenders make apart from the two hearts?

(b) Which card must partner have to defeat the contract?

QUESTIONS

(16)

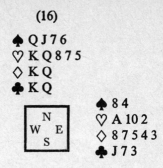

♠ Q J 7 6
♡ K Q 8 7 5
◇ K Q
♣ K Q

```
      N
  W       E
      S
```

♠ 8 4
♡ A 10 2
◇ 8 7 5 4 3
♣ J 7 3

Neither side vulnerable
Dealer: North

South	*North*
—	1 ♡
1 ♠	3 ♠

E/W pass throughout

CONTRACT: 3 ♠.

West leads the ♡ 6.
The ♡ K is played from dummy.
Which card should East play?

ANSWERS

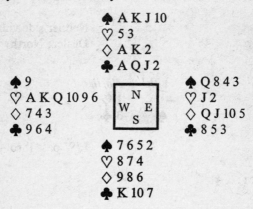

(15)

(*a*) ♠ Q and ♠ 8.

(*b*) ♠ 9.

Declarer is marked with the ♣ K. If West had it, as well as long hearts headed by the A K Q, he wouldn't have passed in the first place. But evidently West had the one card that mattered, the ♠ 9. Otherwise South couldn't have failed to make his contract.

East, of course, did *not* overruff the third heart—the key play—and later made not only his ♠ Q but also the ♠ 8, promoted into a trick by the ruff in dummy.

♠ A K J 10
♡ 5 3
◇ A K 2
♣ A Q J 2

♠ 9
♡ A K Q 10 9 6
◇ 7 4 3
♣ 9 6 4

```
    N
 W     E
    S
```

♠ Q 8 4 3
♡ J 2
◇ Q J 10 5
♣ 8 5 3

♠ 7 6 5 2
♡ 8 7 4
◇ 9 8 6
♣ K 10 7

ANSWERS

(16)

♡ 10.

Can West's ♡ 6 be a singleton? No, for South would then have four hearts, in which case he would have raised North instead of calling 1 ♠.

Can West have four hearts and South a singleton? Again, no, for the six can neither be the fourth highest nor the top of a sequence and West would not make a deceptive lead in this situation.

East should play his partner for a doubleton. Having no entry himself, he must hold up his ace, leaving West a heart to play when he gains the lead.

Note that West is quite likely to have a trump entry, since despite North's strong bidding, South passed 3 ♠.

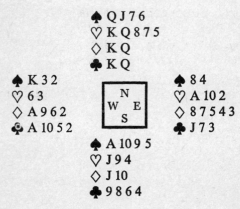

```
              ♠ Q J 7 6
              ♡ K Q 8 7 5
              ◇ K Q
              ♣ K Q
♠ K 3 2                        ♠ 8 4
♡ 6 3              N           ♡ A 10 2
◇ A 9 6 2      W       E       ◇ 8 7 5 4 3
♣ A 10 5 2         S           ♣ J 7 3
              ♠ A 10 9 5
              ♡ J 9 4
              ◇ J 10
              ♣ 9 8 6 4
```

(17)

♠ Q J 7 6
♡ K Q 10 9 6
◇ A K Q
♣ A

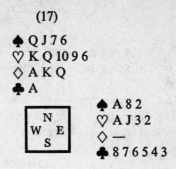

♠ A 8 2
♡ A J 3 2
◇ —
♣ 8 7 6 5 4 3

E/W vulnerable
Dealer: South

South	North
Pass	1 ♡
1 ♠	3 ◇
3 ♡	4 ♠

E/W pass throughout

CONTRACT: 4 ♠.

West leads the ♡ 4.
The ♡ K is played from dummy.
How can East make *certain* of defeating the contract?

(18)

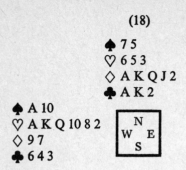

```
            ♠ 7 5
            ♡ 6 5 3
            ◇ A K Q J 2
            ♣ A K 2
♠ A 10
♡ A K Q 10 8 2       ┌─────┐
◇ 9 7                │  N  │
♣ 6 4 3              │ W E │
                     │  S  │
                     └─────┘
```

Neither side vulnerable
Dealer: North

South	West	North	East
—	—	1 ◇	Pass
1 ♠	2 ♡	3 ◇	Pass
3 ♠	Pass	4 ♠	

CONTRACT: 4 ♠.

West leads the ♡ Q, then the ♡ A.

East follows with the ♡ 9 and ♡ 4, and declarer with the ♡ 7 and ♡ J.

(a) Which card should West lead at trick three?

(b) If East has a Yarborough (no honour card), is there any hope of beating the contract? If so, what is it?

ANSWERS

(17)

By going up with the ♡ A and returning the ♡ J, *the key card*. The ♡ 4 is obviously a singleton, but two aces and a ruff come to only three tricks and West cannot have a third trump.

To beat the contract it is essential that West should return a diamond at trick three and to make certain that he does, East, at trick two, leads the ♡ J, an ostentatious card, for he must have lower hearts.

West will read the ♡ J as a SUIT PREFERENCE SIGNAL, calling for the return of a diamond, the *higher-ranking suit*.

SUIT PREFERENCE SIGNALS, named after McKenney in Britain and after Lavinthal in America, were invented by the latter in 1934. They consist in playing an *unnecessarily* high card to call for a higher-ranking suit and an *unnecessarily* low one to direct attention to the lower-ranking suit. Trumps are excluded.

Observe the difference that a diamond return makes on the hand shown below. The defence come to six tricks: two aces, two heart ruffs and two diamond ruffs. Three down. Should West return a club at trick three declarer cannot fail to make his contract.

```
                    ♠ Q J 7 6
                    ♡ K Q 10 9 6
                    ◇ A K Q
                    ♣ A
  ♠ 4 3                          ♠ A 8 2
  ♡ 4             ┌─────────┐    ♡ A J 3 2
  ◇ 7 6 5 4 3 2   │   N     │    ◇ —
  ♣ K J 9 2       │ W   E   │    ♣ 8 7 6 5 4 3
                  │   S     │
                  └─────────┘
                    ♠ K 10 9 5
                    ♡ 8 7 5
                    ◇ J 10 9 8
                    ♣ J 10
```

ANSWERS

(18)

(*a*) ♡ 2.

It is clear that declarer has tricks 'to burn' in the side suits, so he cannot be defeated unless he loses two trump tricks. If partner has an honour in trumps he must be made to play it at trick three. Hence the ♡ 2. The message is unmistakable for West is known to have the ♡ K. If East goes up with the ♠ J (or Q), West will make his ♠ 10.

(*b*) Even if East has no honour, he may have ♠ 9 8 x. He will ruff with the ♠ 8 and force declarer to overruff with one of his three honours. When West comes in with the ♠ A he will lead another heart. East will ruff with the ♠ 9 and force a second honour from declarer. Now West's ♠ 10 will take a trick as the result of two Uppercuts—the name for this type of trump promotion.

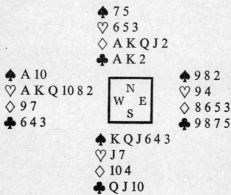

```
                    ♠ 7 5
                    ♡ 6 5 3
                    ◇ A K Q J 2
                    ♣ A K 2
  ♠ A 10                        ♠ 9 8 2
  ♡ A K Q 10 8 2     N          ♡ 9 4
  ◇ 9 7           W     E       ◇ 8 6 5 3
  ♣ 6 4 3            S          ♣ 9 8 7 5
                    ♠ K Q J 6 4 3
                    ♡ J 7
                    ◇ 10 4
                    ♣ Q J 10
```

QUESTIONS

(19)

♠ Q 9 7
♡ 10 4 2
◇ 4
♣ A Q 10 9 8 7

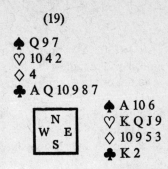

♠ A 10 6
♡ K Q J 9
◇ 10 9 5 3
♣ K 2

Both sides vulnerable
Dealer: South

South	North
1 NT (16–18)	3 NT

E/W pass throughout

CONTRACT: 3 NT.

West leads the ♠ 3.
The ♠ 9 is played from dummy.
Which card should East play?

(20)

♠ 9 7
♡ Q 9 7 4
◇ 6
♣ A Q 10 9 8 7

```
        N        ♠ A J 4
    W       E    ♡ J 10 5 2
        S        ◇ 10 9 5 4
                 ♣ K 2
```

Both sides vulnerable
Dealer: South

South	*North*
1 NT (16–18)	2 ♣ (Stayman)
2 ◇	3 NT

E/W pass throughout

CONTRACT: 3 NT.

West leads the ♠ 3.
Which card should East play?

ANSWERS

(19)

♠ A.

It is *usually* correct to finesse against dummy, but it is *always* correct to break the contract.

Unless West has both the ♠ K and the ♠ J, spades cannot yield enough tricks to defeat 3 NT. But East isn't particularly interested in spades for he can take five tricks himself by switching to a heart at trick two. His ♣ K is a certain entry.

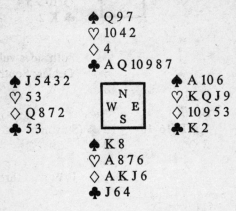

ANSWERS

(20)

♠ J.

If East goes up with the ♠ A—refusing to 'finesse against partner'—declarer will hold up the ♠ K, if he has it, and when East comes in with the ♣ K he will have no spade to return. Expecting West to have the ♠ A, declarer will not hold up his king if East plays the jack.

Playing the jack will cost a trick when West has the ♠ K and declarer's ♠ Q can be caught, but East-West can afford this luxury. Four spades and the ♣ K will suffice to break the contract and West, of course, started with five spades. How do we know? Remember the bidding. South's 2 ◇ response denied a four-card major.

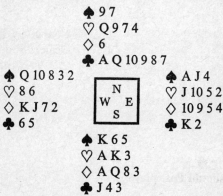

```
                    ♠ 9 7
                    ♡ Q 9 7 4
                    ◇ 6
                    ♣ A Q 10 9 8 7
  ♠ Q 10 8 3 2              ♠ A J 4
  ♡ 8 6          N          ♡ J 10 5 2
  ◇ K J 7 2    W   E        ◇ 10 9 5 4
  ♣ 6 5          S          ♣ K 2
                    ♠ K 6 5
                    ♡ A K 3
                    ◇ A Q 8 3
                    ♣ J 4 3
```

53

QUESTIONS

(21)

♠ 7 6
♡ —
◊ A Q J 10 9
♣ A K Q 7 6 3

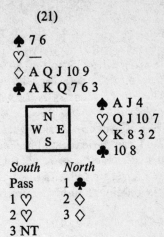

♠ A J 4
♡ Q J 10 7
◊ K 8 3 2
♣ 10 8

South	North
Pass	1 ♣
1 ♡	2 ◊
2 ♡	3 ◊
3 NT	

Neither side vulnerable
Dealer: South
E/W pass throughout

CONTRACT: 3 NT.

West leads the ♠ 3.
Which card should East play?

QUESTIONS

(22)

♠ A J 4
♡ K 3 2
♢ Q J 10 9 8 7
♣ K

```
      N
   W     E
      S
```

♠ K Q 9
♡ A Q J 8
♢ 6
♣ 9 6 5 4 2

E/W vulnerable
Dealer: South

South	North
Pass	1 ♢
2 NT	3 NT

E/W pass throughout

CONTRACT: 3NT.

West leads the ♠ 2.
The ♠ 4 is played from dummy.
(a) Which card should East play to the first trick?
(b) Which card should he play to the second trick?

(21)

♠ A.

There isn't a moment to lose. Seven ready-made tricks are on the table. If declarer has the ♠ K it will be his eighth and the ♡ A will be the ninth.

Couldn't West, not South, have the ♡ A? Possibly, but then West has an entry and there is no purpose in holding up the ♠ A.

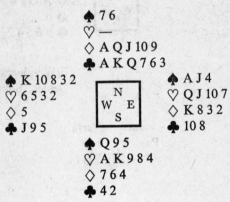

```
              ♠ 7 6
              ♡ —
              ◇ A Q J 10 9
              ♣ A K Q 7 6 3
♠ K 10 8 3 2                    ♠ A J 4
♡ 6 5 3 2          N            ♡ Q J 10 7
◇ 5            W       E        ◇ K 8 3 2
♣ J 9 5            S            ♣ 10 8
              ♠ Q 9 5
              ♡ A K 9 8 4
              ◇ 7 6 4
              ♣ 4 2
```

ANSWERS

(22)

(*a*) ♠ K.

(*b*) ♡ 8.

Unless partner has a quick entry, the contract is unbeatable. South's 2 NT response shows 11–12 points. If they consist of the ◇ A K and the ♣ A, he has nine top tricks. So East should concentrate on the alternative possibility, that South's high cards are the ◇ A and the ♣ A Q J.

East now sees five certain tricks for the defence: one spade, three hearts and West's presumed ◇ K. But it is imperative that when he comes in, West should return a heart, not a spade, and if he sees East's ♠ Q win the first trick, he may take a 'wrong view'. Even the best of partners sometimes do such things.

To ensure that West does not slip, East takes trick one with the ♠ K to conceal the ♠ Q, not from declarer, but from his partner.

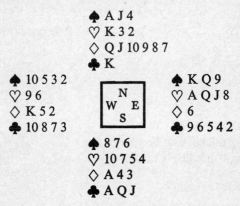

```
            ♠ A J 4
            ♡ K 3 2
            ◇ Q J 10 9 8 7
            ♣ K
♠ 10 5 3 2      N       ♠ K Q 9
♡ 9 6        W     E     ♡ A Q J 8
◇ K 5 2         S       ◇ 6
♣ 10 8 7 3              ♣ 9 6 5 4 2
            ♠ 8 7 6
            ♡ 10 7 5 4
            ◇ A 4 3
            ♣ A Q J
```

(23)

♠ 9
♡ 8 7 2
◇ A K Q 7 4 3
♣ K J 4

```
      N
   W     E
      S
```

♠ A J 7 4
♡ 9 6 5 3
◇ 10 8
♣ 6 5 3

Both sides vulnerable
Dealer: South

South	*North*
1 NT (16–18)	3 NT

E/W pass throughout

CONTRACT: 3 NT.

West leads the ♠ 3.
East plays the ace and South the five.
Which card should East lead to trick two?

(24)

♠ K J 5
♡ K 7
◇ K Q J 10 8 5
♣ Q 5

```
    N
  W   E
    S
```

♠ A Q 6
♡ A Q J
◇ 4 3 2
♣ 8 6 4 3

Neither side vulnerable
Dealer: South

South	North
Pass	1 ◇
1 NT	2 NT
3 NT	

E/W pass throughout

CONTRACT: 3 NT.

West led the ♠ 2.
Declarer played the jack from dummy and went one down.
Which tricks did East take in his own hand and in which order did he take them?

(23)

♠ J.

If East's spades were A J 10 4, there would be no problem, for it would be obvious that the lead back of the ♠ 4—the 'correct' return of the fourth highest—could block the suit. This looks different, but with the ♣ 9 in dummy the position is not dissimilar. To break the contract West must have five spades headed by the K 10 (or the K Q). If East plays back the ♠ 4, the second spade trick will be taken by the 10, the ♠ K will drop the queen and now the jack will block the suit. And if East throws the jack on the king, the ♠ 7 may still block it. All will depend on the ♠ 8. If, after the ♠ K 10, West has nothing better than the ♠ 6, as in the diagram below, all will be lost.

East should foresee the danger when he wins the first trick and avoid blocking the suit by retaining the ♠ 4.

West may be a little uneasy, at first, but one look at dummy will tell him that East cannot have a second ace and that unless the spades yield five tricks quickly, declarer will cruise home in comfort.

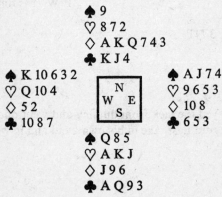

ANSWERS

(24)

♠ A and ♡ A Q J.

East could rely on West to have a certain entry. With 11 points South would have found a stronger response than 1 NT, and if he were missing any one of three cards—the ◇ A, the ♣ A or the ♣ K—he couldn't make nine tricks without giving up the lead.

East had to make sure, however, that when West came in, he returned a heart and not another spade. So he won the first trick with the ♠ A, deliberately misleading his partner. And he returned the ♣ 8, disclaiming all interest in clubs.

Coming in with the ◇ A, West duly returned a heart.

Note that if East wins the first trick with the ♠ Q and West leads a second spade, declarer can make his contract by playing low from dummy.

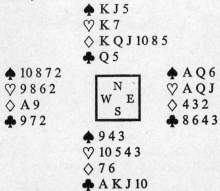

Compare this Quiz with 22. The above is a more advanced variation on the same theme.

QUESTIONS

(25)

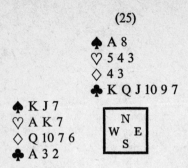

♠ A 8
♡ 5 4 3
♢ 4 3
♣ K Q J 10 9 7

♠ K J 7
♡ A K 7
♢ Q 10 7 6
♣ A 3 2

Neither side vulnerable
Dealer: West

South	West	North	East
—	1 ♢	2 ♣	Pass
2 NT	Pass	3 NT	—

CONTRACT: 3 NT.

West leads the ♡ K.
East plays the ♡ J and declarer the ♡ 6.
Which card should West lead at trick two?

(26)

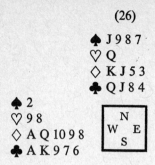

♠ J 9 8 7
♡ Q
◇ K J 5 3
♣ Q J 8 4

♠ 2
♡ 9 8
◇ A Q 10 9 8
♣ A K 9 7 6

N
W E
S

N/S vulnerable
Dealer: West

South	West	North	East
—	1 ◇	Pass	Pass
Dble	2 ♣	Dble	Pass
2 ♠	Pass	3 ♠	Pass
4 ♠			

CONTRACT: 4 ♠.

West leads the ♣ K.

East follows with the ♣ 10 and declarer with the ♣ 3.

At trick two West leads the ◇ A to which East follows with the deuce and declarer with the ◇ 4.

Which tricks will defenders make and in which order will they make them?

(25)

♠ K.

West's main concern should be to knock out dummy's only entry to the clubs. The hearts can wait—a long time. East's ♡ J is certainly encouraging, but it denies the ♡ Q and he can hardly have an entry.

```
                    ♠ A 8
                    ♡ 5 4 3
                    ◇ 4 3
                    ♣ K Q J 10 9 7
  ♠ K J 7                          ♠ 10 9 6 5 2
  ♡ A K 7          N               ♡ J 10 9 2
  ◇ Q 10 7 6    W     E            ◇ 5 2
  ♣ A 3 2          S               ♣ 8 6
                    ♠ Q 4 3
                    ♡ Q 8 6
                    ◇ A K J 9 8
                    ♣ 5 4
```

The play of the ♠ K—an unsupported honour sent on a suicide mission to kill an entry—is known as the Merrimac Coup.

(26)

A diamond, ruffed by East, then the ♣ A and another diamond ruffed by East.

The key to the defence lies in East's pass over 2 ♣ doubled. Had he three diamonds and only two clubs, he would have put West back to diamonds, the suit he bid first. Yet East's ♣ 10 can only be a doubleton (or singleton). What, then, does the ◇ 2 imply? He cannot have three diamonds and with two he would play high-low. So that deuce must be a singleton.

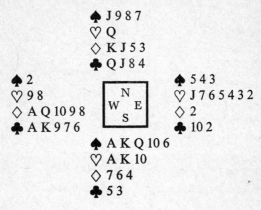

♠ J 9 8 7
♡ Q
◇ K J 5 3
♣ Q J 8 4

♠ 2	♠ 5 4 3
♡ 9 8	♡ J 7 6 5 4 3 2
◇ A Q 10 9 8	◇ 2
♣ A K 9 7 6	♣ 10 2

♠ A K Q 10 6
♡ A K 10
◇ 7 6 4
♣ 5 3

QUESTIONS

(27)

```
                    ♠ A K 10 8 6
                    ♡ 5 2
                    ◇ 9 4 3
                    ♣ Q 3 2
              ┌─────────┐        ♠ Q J 5 4
              │    N    │        ♡ 4 3
              │ W     E │        ◇ 8 7 6
              │    S    │        ♣ 7 6 5 4
              └─────────┘
```

N/S vulnerable
Dealer: South

South	West	North	East
2 ♡	3 ♣	3 ♠	Pass
4 NT	Pass	5 ◇	Pass
6 ♡			

CONTRACT: 6 ♡.

West leads the ♡ A, then the ♡ 6.

Declarer wins and continues with five more rounds of hearts on which West throws: ♣ J, ♣ 8, ♠ 2, ♠ 3, and ◇ 5.

Which should be East's first four discards?

QUESTIONS

(28)

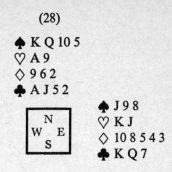

♠ K Q 10 5
♡ A 9
◇ 9 6 2
♣ A J 5 2

          ♠ J 9 8
          ♡ K J
          ◇ 10 8 5 4 3
          ♣ K Q 7

Neither side vulnerable
Dealer: South

South	North
Pass	1 ♣
1 ♡	1 ♠
3 ♡	4 ♡

E/W pass throughout

CONTRACT: 4 ♡.

West leads the ◇ A, then the ◇ K.
Declarer follows with the ◇ 7 and ◇ J.
At trick three West plays the ♣ 10, taken with the ♣ A.
Declarer now leads the ♡ A and the ♡ 9 to East's ♡ K, West playing the ♡ 4, then the ♡ 3.
Five tricks have been played and defenders have won three of them.
Which card should East play at trick six?

(27)

The four clubs.

Since West wouldn't have called 3 ♣ with fewer than five clubs, declarer must have a void or, more likely, the bare A (with ♣ A K, West would have surely played a club). By throwing all his clubs East enables his partner to count the suit and to know which cards to keep to the end.

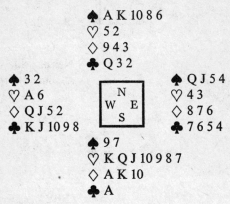

```
                    ♠ A K 10 8 6
                    ♡ 5 2
                    ◇ 9 4 3
                    ♣ Q 3 2
    ♠ 3 2                          ♠ Q J 5 4
    ♡ A 6            ┌─────┐       ♡ 4 3
    ◇ Q J 5 2        │  N  │       ◇ 8 7 6
    ♣ K J 10 9 8     │W   E│       ♣ 7 6 5 4
                     │  S  │
                     └─────┘
                    ♠ 9 7
                    ♡ K Q J 10 9 8 7
                    ◇ A K 10
                    ♣ A
```

The thoughtful reader will have observed that declarer can still make his contract on a squeeze. After playing off his trumps, he crosses to the ♠ A and cashes the ♠ K. That's the squeeze card. Reduced to three cards, West cannot retain the ♣ K and three diamonds. Without seeing the cards, however, South can easily go wrong.

ANSWERS

(28)

A diamond.

West's sequence, the ◇ A first, then the ◇ K, is the conventional method of showing a doubleton,* so East knows that his partner has no more of the suit. But has he a trump? Yes. By playing the ♡ 4 *before* the ♡ 3, West signals three trumps. That again is conventional. Contrary to the practice in the other suits, high-low in trumps shows three and usually indicates a desire to ruff.

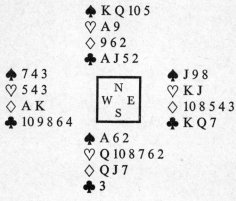

```
              ♠ K Q 10 5
              ♡ A 9
              ◇ 9 6 2
              ♣ A J 5 2
♠ 7 4 3                        ♠ J 9 8
♡ 5 4 3         N             ♡ K J
◇ A K        W     E          ◇ 10 8 5 4 3
♣ 10 9 8 6 4     S             ♣ K Q 7
              ♠ A 6 2
              ♡ Q 10 8 7 6 2
              ◇ Q J 7
              ♣ 3
```

---

* If East-West played the A from a suit headed by the A K—a practice which is gaining in popularity—the reverse would apply. The king, followed by the ace, would then show a doubleton.

QUESTIONS

(29)

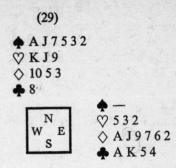

♠ A J 7 5 3 2
♡ K J 9
◇ 10 5 3
♣ 8

♠ —
♡ 5 3 2
◇ A J 9 7 6 2
♣ A K 5 4

N
W E
S

E/W vulnerable
Dealer: West

South	West	North	East
—	Pass	Pass	1 ◇
1 ♡	2 ◇	2 ♡	4 ◇
4 ♡	—		

CONTRACT: 4 ♡.

West leads the ◇ K.
(a) Which card should East play?
(b) If East is on play to trick three—say he ruffed a spade at trick two—which card should he lead?

(30)

♠ Q 10 4 3
♡ 10 6 5 3
◇ K J 10 2
♣ 9

```
      N
   W     E
      S
```

♠ J 9 2
♡ J 2
◇ Q 8 6
♣ Q J 5 4 3

Neither side vulnerable
Dealer: South

South	*North*
1 NT (12–14)	2 ♣ (Stayman)
2 ♡	

E/W pass throughout

CONTRACT: 2 ♡.

West leads the ♠ K.
Which card should East play?

ANSWERS

(29)

(*a*) ◇ J.

(*b*) A low club.

If East wants partner to lead a second diamond he can encourage him without being ostentatious. The 9 or 7 will convey the message. The ◇ J is blatant, an *unnecessarily* high card and therefore a signal, calling on West to switch to spades, the higher-ranking suit. If East wanted a club, he would play the ◇ 2.

How can the contract be beaten? Since West supported diamonds, the suit cannot be expected to yield another trick. All East can see for the defence is: the ◇ K, a spade ruff and one club—unless he can put partner in to lead another spade. The only hope lies in under-leading the ♣ A K. West may have the ♣ Q or else, if declarer has the queen, he may be 'asleep' and play low. Such things have been known to happen—even among the best people.

It is true that as things are, East-West can make 6 ◇, but that's no reason for allowing North-South to make 4 ♡.

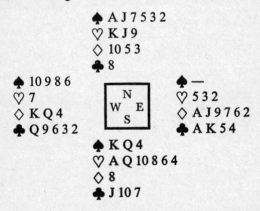

```
              ♠ A J 7 5 3 2
              ♡ K J 9
              ◇ 10 5 3
              ♣ 8
  ♠ 10 9 8 6        N        ♠ —
  ♡ 7          W       E     ♡ 5 3 2
  ◇ K Q 4           S        ◇ A J 9 7 6 2
  ♣ Q 9 6 3 2                ♣ A K 5 4
              ♠ K Q 4
              ♡ A Q 10 8 6 4
              ◇ 8
              ♣ J 10 7
```

ANSWERS

♠ 9.

East wants a spade continuation for two reasons:

1. A switch to any other suit may cost a trick.
2. Seeing the high-low signal, declarer may well think that East has a doubleton and will ruff the third spade. Deciding not to 'waste' his queen, he may play the ♠ 10, allowing the defence to collect three spade tricks.

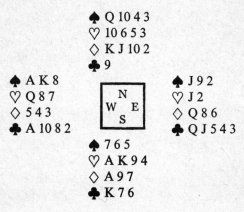

```
                    ♠ Q 10 4 3
                    ♡ 10 6 5 3
                    ◇ K J 10 2
                    ♣ 9
    ♠ A K 8                         ♠ J 9 2
    ♡ Q 8 7        ┌─────────┐      ♡ J 2
    ◇ 5 4 3        │    N    │      ◇ Q 8 6
    ♣ A 10 8 2     │  W   E  │      ♣ Q J 5 4 3
                   │    S    │
                   └─────────┘
                    ♠ 7 6 5
                    ♡ A K 9 4
                    ◇ A 9 7
                    ♣ K 7 6
```

QUESTIONS

(31)

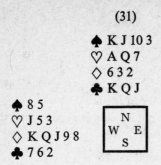

♠ K J 10 3
♡ A Q 7
◇ 6 3 2
♣ K Q J

♠ 8 5
♡ J 5 3
◇ K Q J 9 8
♣ 7 6 2

```
    N
 W     E
    S
```

Both sides vulnerable
Dealer: North

South	North
—	1 NT (16–18)
3 ♠	4 ♠
5 ◇	5 ♡
6 ♠	

E/W pass throughout

CONTRACT: 6 ♠.

West leads the ◇ K.

Declarer wins with the ace, crosses to dummy with a trump and ruffs a diamond. He goes back to dummy with another trump—East throws a club—and ruffs dummy's last diamond. Three rounds of clubs follow, declarer ending in his hand with the ♣ A.

Eight cards have been played—two trumps, three diamonds and three clubs. Declarer now leads the ♡ 2.

Which four cards should make up this (ninth) trick?

74

QUESTIONS

(32)

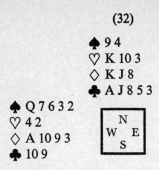

♠ 9 4
♡ K 10 3
◇ K J 8
♣ A J 8 5 3

♠ Q 7 6 3 2
♡ 4 2
◇ A 10 9 3
♣ 10 9

Neither side vulnerable
Dealer: South

South	North
1 ♡	2 ♣
2 ♡	4 ♡

E/W pass throughout

CONTRACT: 4 ♡.

West leads the ♣ 10.
A low club is played from dummy and East wins with the ♣ K.
He returns the ◇ 7 to which declarer follows with the deuce.
Which card should West play?

(31)

♡ 2, ♡ J, ♡ Q and ♡ K.

If declarer had the ♡ K, he would have thirteen tricks. So East must have it. If West plays low, declarer will insert dummy's ♡ 7 and East will be end-played—forced to lead away from his ♡ K or to concede a ruff and discard. West must, therefore, go up with the ♡ J. The finesse loses.

If declarer has the ♡ 10 or the ♡ 9 he will still make his slam, but at least it won't be West's fault. If he fails to go up with the ♡ J, it will be.

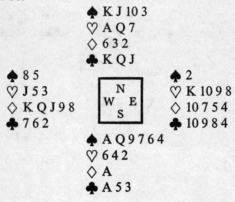

ANSWERS

(32)

$\diamond$ 9.

That diamond switch is promising. East must have a good reason for returning a diamond in preference to a spade. South's 2 $\heartsuit$ rebid showed a minimum, so East may have the $\heartsuit$ A. By itself that won't be enough to defeat the contract, but it may prove to be a vital entry, paving the way for a diamond ruff.

Can the $\diamond$ 7 be a singleton? Unlikely, for with $\diamond$ Q x x x x South's rebid would have been 2 $\diamond$ rather than 2 $\heartsuit$. Could East have $\diamond$ Q x x? Again unlikely for he would have led his lowest and with the 10, 9 and 8 on view, the seven can't be that.

So East has a doubleton diamond and West must hold up his ace to keep communications open with his partner. When East comes in with the $\heartsuit$ A he will have a diamond left to put West in—and he will get his ruff.

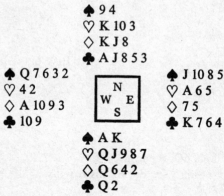

```
                    ♠ 9 4
                    ♡ K 10 3
                    ◇ K J 8
                    ♣ A J 8 5 3
 ♠ Q 7 6 3 2                        ♠ J 10 8 5
 ♡ 4 2          ┌─────────┐        ♡ A 6 5
 ◇ A 10 9 3     │    N    │        ◇ 7 5
 ♣ 10 9         │ W     E │        ♣ K 7 6 4
                │    S    │
                └─────────┘
                    ♠ A K
                    ♡ Q J 9 8 7
                    ◇ Q 6 4 2
                    ♣ Q 2
```

QUESTIONS

(33)

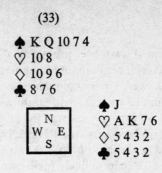

♠ K Q 10 7 4
♡ 10 8
◇ 10 9 6
♣ 8 7 6

♠ J
♡ A K 7 6
◇ 5 4 3 2
♣ 5 4 3 2

Neither side vulnerable
Dealer: South

South	North
2 ♠	4 ♠
6 ♠	

E/W pass throughout

CONTRACT: 6 ♠.

West leads the ♡ Q, then the ♡ J.

Declarer ruffs and leads out all his trumps, West showing out on the first round.

Which should be East's first five discards?

QUESTIONS

(34)

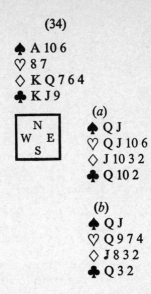

♠ A 10 6
♡ 8 7
♢ K Q 7 6 4
♣ K J 9

(a)
♠ Q J
♡ Q J 10 6
♢ J 10 3 2
♣ Q 10 2

(b)
♠ Q J
♡ Q 9 7 4
♢ J 8 3 2
♣ Q 3 2

Neither side vulnerable
Dealer: South

South	North
1 NT (12–14)	3 NT

E/W pass throughout

CONTRACT: 3 NT.

West leads the ♠ 4.
The ♠ 6 is played from dummy.
Which card should East play?

(33)

East should throw his four clubs, then a diamond—or four diamonds and then a club.

As soon as he passes from one minor to the other, his partner will know that he has no more of the first and this will tell him what to keep. To throw a heart, or to discard from each minor in turn, would be sadly uninformative.

Since declarer has shown up with a singleton heart and seven spades, he is known to have five cards in the minors. East cannot hope for a trick in either himself, but he has a vital part to play by helping West to count declarer's hand.

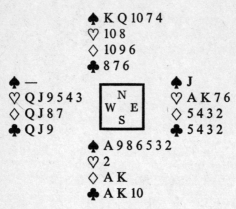

♠ K Q 10 7 4
♡ 10 8
◇ 10 9 6
♣ 8 7 6

♠ —
♡ Q J 9 5 4 3
◇ Q J 8 7
♣ Q J 9

♠ J
♡ A K 7 6
◇ 5 4 3 2
♣ 5 4 3 2

♠ A 9 8 6 5 3 2
♡ 2
◇ A K
♣ A K 10

(34)

(*a*) ♠ Q.
(*b*) ♠ J.

In following to partner's suit it is correct to play the lower of touching honours. The unnatural play of the higher honour in (*a*) will deceive partner, but it will deceive declarer too, and if he has the ♠ K, partner will readily forgive the deception. Should partner have the ♠ K himself, the ♠ Q will hold the trick, the ♠ J will follow and all will be well.

There is another consideration. If declarer has the ♠ K, West may win the first trick for the defence. Seeing no future in spades, he may well switch to a heart or a club and either will suit East.

In (*b*) a switch might be unfortunate and East has no wish to discourage a spade continuation.

(35)

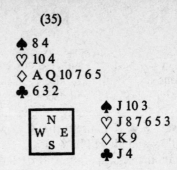

♠ 8 4
♡ 10 4
◇ A Q 10 7 6 5
♣ 6 3 2

♠ J 10 3
♡ J 8 7 6 5 3
◇ K 9
♣ J 4

Neither side vulnerable
Dealer: South

South	North
1 ♣	1 ◇
3 NT	

E/W pass throughout

CONTRACT: 3 NT.

West leads the ♠ 7.

East plays the ♠ 10 and declarer, winning with the ♠ K, lays down the ♣ A. Then he runs the ◇ J.

(a) If West follows with the ◇ 2, which card should East play?

(b) If West follows with the ◇ 8, which card should East play?

QUESTIONS

(36)

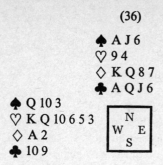

♠ A J 6
♡ 9 4
◇ K Q 8 7
♣ A Q J 6

♠ Q 10 3
♡ K Q 10 6 5 3
◇ A 2
♣ 10 9

```
    N
  W   E
    S
```

Neither side vulnerable
Dealer: South

South	*West*	*North*	*East*
Pass	1 ♡	Dble	Pass
1 ♠	Pass	2 ♠	Pass
2 NT	Pass	3 NT	

CONTRACT: 3 NT.

West leads the ♡ K and holds the trick.
East's card is the ♡ 8 and declarer's the ♡ 7.

(a) Which card should West play at trick two?
  After winning his first trick, declarer leads the ♠ 4, successfully finesses the jack and continues with the ♠ A.

(b) Which card should West play?

ANSWERS

(35)

(*a*) ◇ K.

(*b*) ◇ K.

Whether West has two diamonds or three, this is no time for a daring hold-up play. Apply the Rule of Eleven.

Four cards higher than the ♠ 7 (11–7=4) are missing from West's hand. East can see three of them, leaving one only for declarer and he has produced it already, the ♠ K. So all West's spades are good and the lead of the ♠ 7 suggests a five-card suit.

When a contract can be broken the simple way, there is no need to be subtle. And it may be dangerous. If South needs two diamond tricks only, he won't finesse again.

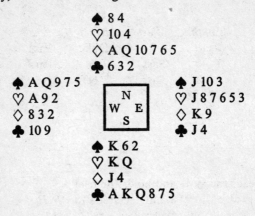

ANSWERS

(36)

(*a*) ♣ 10.

(*b*) ♠ Q.

East's ♡ 8 is surely a singleton, for had he the jack—or the ace—he would have played it. He knows that West would not lead the K from K Q unless he had the ten, too.

Declarer's ♡ 7 must be a false card designed to induce another heart from West into his A J tenace. This is known as the Bath Coup—the most elementary of the many plays described as a Coup.

Since the jack wins the first trick in spades, declarer knows that West has the queen, but he does not know about the ten. With the jack out of the way, the queen and ten are equals. Therefore, West should play the card he is known to have and conceal the other. With the K 9 in the closed hand, declarer may finesse—and lose to the ♠ 10. He may do no such thing, of course, but at least he is put to a guess.

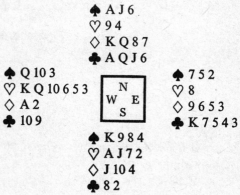

```
              ♠ A J 6
              ♡ 9 4
              ◇ K Q 8 7
              ♣ A Q J 6
♠ Q 10 3                        ♠ 7 5 2
♡ K Q 10 6 5 3      N           ♡ 8
◇ A 2           W     E         ◇ 9 6 5 3
♣ 10 9              S           ♣ K 7 5 4 3
              ♠ K 9 8 4
              ♡ A J 7 2
              ◇ J 10 4
              ♣ 8 2
```

QUESTIONS

(37)

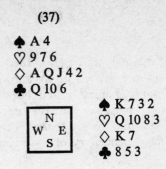

♠ A 4
♡ 9 7 6
♢ A Q J 4 2
♣ Q 10 6

♠ K 7 3 2
♡ Q 10 8 3
♢ K 7
♣ 8 5 3

```
      N
   W     E
      S
```

Neither side vulnerable
Dealer: South

South	North
1 ♣	1 ♢
1 NT	3 NT

E/W pass throughout

CONTRACT: 3 NT.

West leads the ♠ 5.

The ♠ 4 is played from dummy and East wins with the king, declarer following with the ♠ 8.

Which card should East play at trick two?

QUESTIONS

(38)

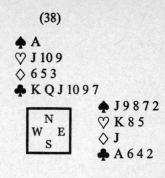

♠ A
♡ J 10 9
◇ 6 5 3
♣ K Q J 10 9 7

♠ J 9 8 7 2
♡ K 8 5
◇ J
♣ A 6 4 2

Neither side vulnerable
Dealer: North

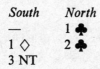

South	North
—	1 ♣
1 ◇	2 ♣
3 NT	

E/W pass throughout

CONTRACT: 3 NT.

West led the ♡ 6.
The ♡ K won the first trick, declarer following with the deuce.
East misdefended and the contract was made.
What mistake did East make?

ANSWERS

(37)

♡ 10.

Since East can see all the spades below the five, West's lead indicates a four-card suit, so that even if he has the queen, spades will yield no more than three tricks. Worse still, if West has the ♣ Q, he is unlikely to have another worthwhile card,* and the contract is probably unbeatable.

Should West have the ♡ K, however, the defence can take three hearts and the ◇ K will then be the setting trick. East has little to lose and much to gain by leading his ♡ 10 which will trap declarer's jack if the cards are distributed as in the diagram below. His ♡ Q 8, a deadly tenace over dummy's 9 7, will win two more tricks.

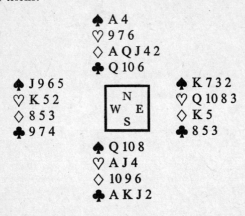

```
                    ♠ A 4
                    ♡ 9 7 6
                    ◇ A Q J 4 2
                    ♣ Q 10 6
  ♠ J 9 6 5                        ♠ K 7 3 2
  ♡ K 5 2          ┌─────────┐     ♡ Q 10 8 3
  ◇ 8 5 3          │   N     │     ◇ K 5
  ♣ 9 7 4          │ W   E   │     ♣ 8 5 3
                   │   S     │
                   └─────────┘
                    ♠ Q 10 8
                    ♡ A J 4
                    ◇ 10 9 6
                    ♣ A K J 2
```

---

* Playing a weak (12–14) non-vulnerable 1 NT, a *rebid* of 1 NT, as here, promises 15–16 points.

ANSWERS

(38)

East played a spade at trick two.

Evidently he couldn't wait to knock out dummy's only entry to those powerful clubs.

Was that so bad? Isn't the situation similar to the one in Quiz 25 when a defender had to sacrifice a king (the Merrimac Coup) to kill an entry to dummy's long suit?

The basic difference between the two hands is that in Quiz 25 the defence couldn't win the first four (or five) tricks. Here they can.

East should have applied the Rule of Eleven. West's lead was the ♡ 6. So there were five (11–6=5) hearts higher than the six in the other three hands and East could see them all—three in dummy, two in his own hand—leaving none for declarer. It follows that West could take all his hearts without surrendering the lead.

The entry-killing play couldn't run away. The contract could—and did.

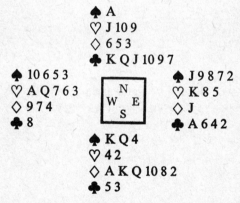

```
                    ♠ A
                    ♡ J 10 9
                    ◇ 6 5 3
                    ♣ K Q J 10 9 7
  ♠ 10 6 5 3                        ♠ J 9 8 7 2
  ♡ A Q 7 6 3      N                ♡ K 8 5
  ◇ 9 7 4       W     E             ◇ J
  ♣ 8              S                ♣ A 6 4 2
                    ♠ K Q 4
                    ♡ 4 2
                    ◇ A K Q 10 8 2
                    ♣ 5 3
```

(39)

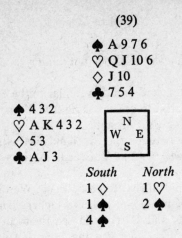

♠ A 9 7 6
♡ Q J 10 6
◇ J 10
♣ 7 5 4

♠ 4 3 2
♡ A K 4 3 2
◇ 5 3
♣ A J 3

	N	
W		E
	S	

South	North
1 ◇	1 ♡
1 ♠	2 ♠
4 ♠	

E/W vulnerable
Dealer: South
E/W pass throughout

CONTRACT: 4 ♠.

West leads the ♡ K.
East follows with the ♡ 5 and declarer with the ♡ 7.
Which card should West lead at trick two?

QUESTIONS

(40)

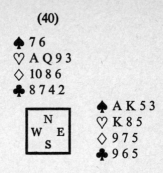

♠ 7 6
♡ A Q 9 3
◇ 10 8 6
♣ 8 7 4 2

♠ A K 5 3
♡ K 8 5
◇ 9 7 5
♣ 9 6 5

Neither side vulnerable
Dealer: South

South bids 1 NT (12–14) and all pass.

CONTRACT: 1 NT.

West leads the ♠ 2.
Which card should East play at trick two?

(39)

♣ 3.

East's ♡ 5 is ominous. It looks like the lowest of three rather than like a singleton, and if so, declarer has no more hearts. Where, then, can the defence find another three tricks?

The trump position seems thoroughly unpromising and should South need a finesse in diamonds, West knows that it will succeed. Only in clubs can there be a future, but time presses, for given the chance, declarer will get rid of a club (or two clubs) from dummy on his diamonds.

As so often in defence, the key to success lies in wishful thinking. To beat the contract partner must have the ♣ K. Play him for it—and hope.

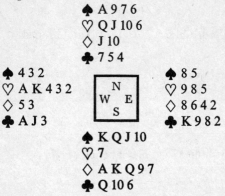

```
              ♠ A 9 7 6
              ♡ Q J 10 6
              ◇ J 10
              ♣ 7 5 4
  ♠ 4 3 2          N          ♠ 8 5
  ♡ A K 4 3 2   W     E       ♡ 9 8 5
  ◇ 5 3            S          ◇ 8 6 4 2
  ♣ A J 3                     ♣ K 9 8 2
              ♠ K Q J 10
              ♡ 7
              ◇ A K Q 9 7
              ♣ Q 10 6
```

ANSWERS

(40)

♠ 3.

West's lead indicates a four-card suit, probably headed by the jack. If so, declarer has ♠ Q x x, maybe Q 10 x, and if he can be induced to make the wrong guess, the defence will take four spade tricks.

Winning the first trick with the ♠ A, East returns the ♠ 3, creating the impression that West has the ♠ K.

Declarer may still go up with the ♠ Q. He will doubtless do so, unless he has the ten as well, but East runs no risk. He will be in again shortly with the ♡ K, in good time to cash his ♠ K. West is marked with 10 points or so on the bidding, so no entry problem is likely to arise.

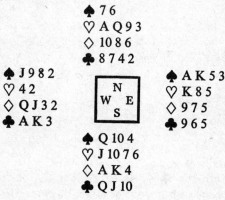

```
              ♠ 7 6
              ♡ A Q 9 3
              ◇ 10 8 6
              ♣ 8 7 4 2
♠ J 9 8 2                    ♠ A K 5 3
♡ 4 2          N            ♡ K 8 5
◇ Q J 3 2   W     E         ◇ 9 7 5
♣ A K 3        S            ♣ 9 6 5
              ♠ Q 10 4
              ♡ J 10 7 6
              ◇ A K 4
              ♣ Q J 10
```

QUESTIONS

(41)

```
              ♠ A K 7
              ♡ 6 5 4 3
              ◇ J 10 7
              ♣ A K 9
♠ Q J 6 5     ┌─────────┐
♡ K 9 8       │    N    │
◇ A Q         │  W   E  │
♣ Q J 10 3    │    S    │
              └─────────┘
```

Neither side vulnerable
Dealer: West

South	West	North	East
—	1 ♠	Dble	2 ♠
4 ◇	Pass	5 ◇	

CONTRACT: 5 ◇.

West leads the ♣ Q.

Winning with the ♣ K, declarer plays the ace and king of spades, discarding a heart on the second round, ruffs a spade in the closed hand and crosses to dummy with the ♣ A.

At trick six declarer runs the ◇ J to West's queen. East follows with the ◇ 3.

Which card should West lead at trick seven?

(42)

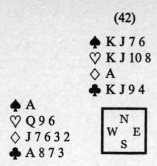

♠ K J 7 6
♡ K J 10 8
◇ A
♣ K J 9 4

♠ A
♡ Q 9 6
◇ J 7 6 3 2
♣ A 8 7 3

Neither side vulnerable
Dealer: North

South	North
—	1 ♣
1 ♠	3 ♠
4 ♠	

E/W pass throughout

CONTRACT: 4 ♠.

West leads the ◇ 3 to dummy's ace.
At trick two declarer plays a spade.
(a) Which card should West lead at trick three?
(b) Which tricks does he hope to make to beat the contract and
in which order does he hope to make them?

(41)

♢ A.

If West tries to cash his ♣ J, declarer will ruff and throw West in with the ♢ A, forcing him to play away from his ♡ K or to lead a black card, conceding a ruff and discard.

Seeing declarer eliminate spades, West should be wary of being end-played. To avert the threat he must play off the ♢ A quickly —while he still has a safe *exit card*.

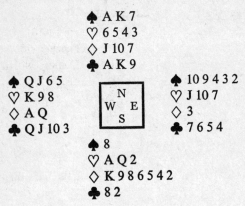

Note that declarer didn't give himself the best chance. On the bidding, West was pretty certain to have the ♢ A. So instead of using the ♣ A, his last entry to dummy, to take the trump finesse, declarer should have eliminated clubs, as well as spades, and played the ♢ K from his hand. Unless West had all three trumps, the contract would now be foolproof.

(42)

(*a*) A low club.

(*b*) ♣ Q; ♣ A; club ruff by East.

East can't have much on the bidding, but he may just produce the ♣ Q and if it's a doubleton, it may be enough.

No other defence offers better prospects.

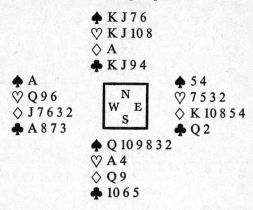

```
                    ♠ K J 7 6
                    ♡ K J 10 8
                    ◇ A
                    ♣ K J 9 4
        ♠ A                         ♠ 5 4
        ♡ Q 9 6          N          ♡ 7 5 3 2
        ◇ J 7 6 3 2   W     E       ◇ K 10 8 5 4
        ♣ A 8 7 3         S         ♣ Q 2
                    ♠ Q 10 9 8 3 2
                    ♡ A 4
                    ◇ Q 9
                    ♣ 10 6 5
```

(43)

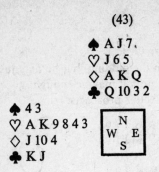

♠ A J 7
♡ J 6 5
◇ A K Q
♣ Q 10 3 2

♠ 4 3
♡ A K 9 8 4 3
◇ J 10 4
♣ K J

N
W   E
S

Both sides vulnerable
Dealer: West

South	West	North	East
—	1 ♡	Dble	2 ♡
4 ♠			

CONTRACT: 4 ♠.

West leads the ♡ K.
East plays the ♡ 10 and declarer the ♡ 7.
Which card should West lead at trick two?

QUESTIONS

(44)

♠ 8 7 2
♡ 6 5
♢ A K Q 10 9
♣ J 9 7

♠ K 10 9 6 3
♡ A K 7
♢ J 8
♣ 5 3 2

```
      N
   W     E
      S
```

Both sides vulnerable
Dealer: South

South	West	North	East
1 ♡	1 ♠	2 ♢	Pass
4 ♡			

CONTRACT: 4 ♡.

West leads the ♡ K and all follow.
How should West continue?

♣ K.

East wouldn't have raised the 1 ♡ opening on a doubleton, so declarer cannot have another heart. If he has the ♣ A, the contract is unbeatable, even if partner turns up with a trump trick. But should East have the ♣ A, and it's not unlikely, West can get a ruff—and defeat the contract.

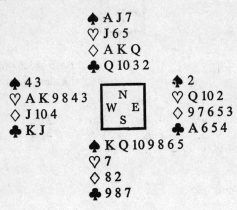

```
                    ♠ A J 7
                    ♡ J 6 5
                    ◇ A K Q
                    ♣ Q 10 3 2
  ♠ 4 3                           ♠ 2
  ♡ A K 9 8 4 3     N             ♡ Q 10 2
  ◇ J 10 4       W     E          ◇ 9 7 6 5 3
  ♣ K J             S             ♣ A 6 5 4
                    ♠ K Q 10 9 8 6 5
                    ♡ 7
                    ◇ 8 2
                    ♣ 9 8 7
```

(44)

A diamond.

If declarer has three diamonds the prospects of beating the contract seem negligible, for to justify his 4 ♡ bid he must have the ♠ A and the ♣ A K. If, however, he has two diamonds only, he can be cut off from dummy. West will play a second diamond when he comes in with the ♡ A and then maybe declarer will be unable to find ten tricks all on his own—as in the diagram below.

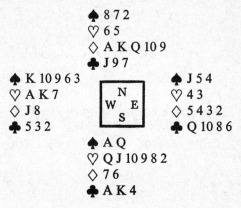

```
            ♠ 8 7 2
            ♡ 6 5
            ◇ A K Q 10 9
            ♣ J 9 7
♠ K 10 9 6 3        ♠ J 5 4
♡ A K 7      N      ♡ 4 3
◇ J 8     W   E     ◇ 5 4 3 2
♣ 5 3 2      S      ♣ Q 10 8 6
            ♠ A Q
            ♡ Q J 10 9 8 2
            ◇ 7 6
            ♣ A K 4
```

QUESTIONS

(45)

♠ 9 6
♡ A 8 5
◇ K J
♣ K J 9 5 3 2

```
      N
  W       E
      S
```

♠ K Q J 10 2
♡ 7 3
◇ A Q 3 2
♣ 10 4

Neither side vulnerable
Dealer: East

South	West	North	East
			1 ♠
2 ♡	2 ♠	4 ♡	

CONTRACT: 4 ♡.

West leads the ♠ A.
What card should East play?

QUESTIONS

(46)

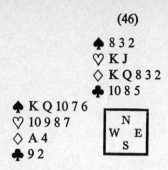

♠ 8 3 2
♡ K J
◇ K Q 8 3 2
♣ 10 8 5

♠ K Q 10 7 6
♡ 10 9 8 7
◇ A 4
♣ 9 2

N/S vulnerable
Dealer: South

South	North
1 NT (16–18)	3 NT

E/W pass throughout

CONTRACT: 3 NT.

West leads the ♠ K.
East plays the ♠ J and declarer the ♠ 5.
Which card should West play at trick two?

ANSWERS

(45)

♠ K.

If East simply wanted another spade he could find an encouraging card without being ostentatious. The king is an *unnecessarily* high card and therefore a SUIT PREFERENCE SIGNAL, calling for a switch to the higher-ranking suit.

Left to himself, West would probably lead his singleton club. Seeing the ♠ K, West switches to a diamond—the one way to break the contract.

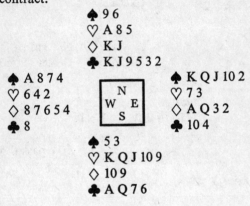

```
                    ♠ 9 6
                    ♡ A 8 5
                    ◇ K J
                    ♣ K J 9 5 3 2
  ♠ A 8 7 4                           ♠ K Q J 10 2
  ♡ 6 4 2              N              ♡ 7 3
  ◇ 8 7 6 5 4      W       E          ◇ A Q 3 2
  ♣ 8                  S              ♣ 10 4
                    ♠ 5 3
                    ♡ K Q J 10 9
                    ◇ 10 9
                    ♣ A Q 7 6
```

ANSWERS

(46)

♠ Q.

East's ♠ J should not be confused with a SUIT PREFERENCE SIGNAL. He knows that West's lead is probably from a suit headed by the K Q 10 and that he may switch if he doesn't see the jack. After all, with A J x declarer would naturally hold up his ace—the so-called Bath Coup (see Quiz 36)—and West would then look very foolish if he led a second spade.

It follows that far from being an *unnecessarily* high card, that ♠ J is very necessary indeed. Therefore it is not a S.P.S. When in doubt, and especially at trick one, always look on a high card as encouraging, not as signalling suit preference.

Can East's ♠ J be a singleton? Impossible. With A 9 5 4 and the eight in dummy, declarer would win the first trick.

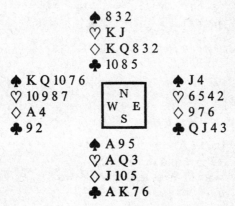

```
                    ♠ 8 3 2
                    ♡ K J
                    ◇ K Q 8 3 2
                    ♣ 10 8 5
     ♠ K Q 10 7 6       ┌─────┐        ♠ J 4
     ♡ 10 9 8 7         │  N  │        ♡ 6 5 4 2
     ◇ A 4            W │     │ E      ◇ 9 7 6
     ♣ 9 2              │  S  │        ♣ Q J 4 3
                        └─────┘
                    ♠ A 9 5
                    ♡ A Q 3
                    ◇ J 10 5
                    ♣ A K 7 6
```

QUESTIONS

(47)

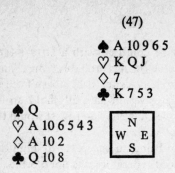

♠ A 10 9 6 5
♡ K Q J
♢ 7
♣ K 7 5 3

♠ Q
♡ A 10 6 5 4 3
♢ A 10 2
♣ Q 10 8

```
      N
  W       E
      S
```

Both sides vulnerable
Dealer: South

South	West	North	East
Pass	1 ♡	1 ♠	Dble
2 ♢			

CONTRACT: 2 ♢.

West leads the ♡ A.
East plays the ♡ 2 and declarer the ♡ 9.
Which card should West lead at trick two?

(48)

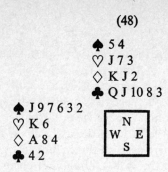

♠ 5 4
♡ J 7 3
◇ K J 2
♣ Q J 10 8 3

♠ J 9 7 6 3 2
♡ K 6
◇ A 8 4
♣ 4 2

Neither side vulnerable
Dealer: South

South bids I NT (12–14) and all pass.

CONTRACT: 1 NT.

West leads the ♠ 6.
East plays the ♠ Q, which holds, and continues with the ♠ K.
Winning with the ♠ A, declarer leads the ◇ 10.
Which card should West play?

ANSWERS

(47)

♡ 10.

A double of an overcall at the one level isn't so much a get-rich-quick scheme as a warning of a misfit. That deuce of hearts looks, therefore, suspiciously like a singleton. To encourage a spade return West leads the ♡ 10. East ruffs and plays a spade, but though declarer leads a trump at once, he is in trouble. East ruffs another heart and plays the ♠ K. If declarer ruffs high, West's ◇ 10 is promoted and there are still three clubs to lose. Should declarer throw a club on the ♠ K and another on the ♠ J, he fares no better. East cashes the ♣ A and goes back to spades. West's ◇ 10 again takes a trick. Maybe someone should have doubled.

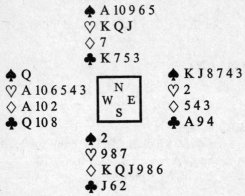

ANSWERS

(48)

♦ A.

If declarer is allowed to make the ♦ K he will have stolen his seventh trick.

West should ask himself: why is declarer concerned with diamonds when the clubs look so much more attractive? The answer must be that the clubs require no attention. It follows that declarer has the ♣ A and ♣ K himself and therefore six-ready-made tricks in the black suits.

West should go up at once with the ♦ A, cash five spades and lead a heart to his partner's ace, beating the contract by two tricks.

East simply must have the ♡ A. Having revealed 7 points already—4 in spades and 7, by inference, in clubs—another ace would make the South hand too strong for a non-vulnerable 1 NT.

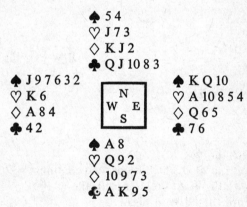

```
              ♠ 5 4
              ♡ J 7 3
              ♦ K J 2
              ♣ Q J 10 8 3
♠ J 9 7 6 3 2           ♠ K Q 10
♡ K 6         N         ♡ A 10 8 5 4
♦ A 8 4     W   E       ♦ Q 6 5
♣ 4 2         S         ♣ 7 6
              ♠ A 8
              ♡ Q 9 2
              ♦ 10 9 7 3
              ♣ A K 9 5
```

QUESTIONS

(49)

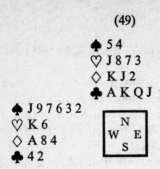

♠ 5 4
♡ J 8 7 3
◇ K J 2
♣ A K Q J

♠ J 9 7 6 3 2
♡ K 6
◇ A 8 4
♣ 4 2

```
    N
 W     E
    S
```

Neither side vulnerable
Dealer: North

South	North
—	1 ♣
1 NT	

E/W pass throughout

CONTRACT: 1 NT.

West leads the ♠ 6.
East plays the ♠ Q which holds, and continues with the ♠ K.
Winning with the ♠ A, declarer leads the ◇ 10.
Which card should West play?

QUESTIONS

(50)

♠ J 4
♡ A Q 3 2
◇ K Q 2
♣ A K Q 2

♠ A K Q 10
♡ 10 9 8 6
◇ J 5 4
♣ J 6

	N	
W		E
	S	

Neither side vulnerable
Dealer: West

South	North
—	1 ♣
1 ◇	2 ♡
2 NT	3 NT

E/W pass throughout

CONTRACT: 3 NT.

West led the ♠ K.

East played the ♠ 9. West continued spades, East following all
the way. Declarer, who had three spades, threw a club on the
fourth round, discarding two hearts from dummy.

At trick five West led a heart.

South had a sub-minimum for his 1 ◇ response and an un-
inspiring 3–3–4–3 shape, yet he made his contract.

Could West have stopped him? If so, how?

111

ANSWERS

(49)

$\diamondsuit$ 4.

If West goes up with the $\diamondsuit$ A he will be presenting declarer with his seventh trick.

Compare this example with the last one. Then, relying on East for the $\heartsuit$ A, West could make certain of beating the contract, while declarer needed only one more trick to make it.

Who has the $\heartsuit$ A this time? Almost certainly South, but if not, he must have the $\diamondsuit$ Q, for with the $\spadesuit$ A and no other honour card, he would have passed 1 $\clubsuit$.

If declarer has the $\heartsuit$ A, West cannot beat the contract on his own, while if the $\diamondsuit$ Q is behind the jack, one diamond trick won't be enough to ensure it.

Either way, West should play the $\diamondsuit$ 4, giving declarer a chance to play low from dummy, in case East has the $\diamondsuit$ Q.

Note that South cannot have the $\diamondsuit$ Q as well as two aces. That would be too much for his 1 NT response, even though some players insist on 8–9 points for a bid of 1 NT over 1 $\clubsuit$.

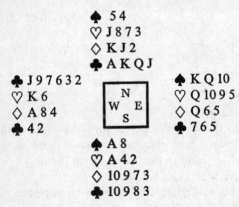

ANSWERS

(50)

West should have switched to a heart at trick three.

In playing the hand, declarer couldn't go wrong. He knew that West, who had passed as dealer, couldn't have the ♡ K as well as the top spades, so he didn't attempt a finesse foredoomed to fail. He went up with the ♡ A and took his four diamonds. He only had 5 points for his bid, but one of them was the ♡ J and that was enough.

Had West looked for the fifth trick, before cashing precipitately the other four, he would have realized that the contract was un-beatable if declarer had either the ♡ K or four clubs. And if East had both, what could he safely discard on the fourth diamond, except a spade? By depriving him of that spade West engineered a deadly squeeze* against his partner. A heart switch—before the third trick—would have left East with one spade to throw on the fourth diamond and another to play back to West later.

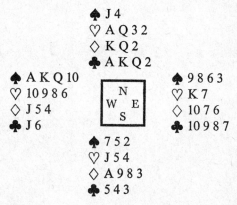

```
              ♠ J 4
              ♡ A Q 3 2
              ◇ K Q 2
              ♣ A K Q 2
♠ A K Q 10                    ♠ 9 8 6 3
♡ 10 9 8 6        N           ♡ K 7
◇ J 5 4       W     E         ◇ 10 7 6
♣ J 6            S            ♣ 10 9 8 7
              ♠ 7 5 2
              ♡ J 5 4
              ◇ A 9 8 3
              ♣ 5 4 3
```

This example is a good deal harder than any of those which have gone before, and that is as it should be, for in the pages

---

* The Vienna Coup: an unblocking play preparatory to a squeeze. A master (the ♡ A in the diagram) is played off. Dummy's other heart(s) can now be discarded, but the threat to the defender with the next highest card (East with the ♡ K) remains. It now comes from the closed hand (♡ J).

In the example above declarer throws the ♡ Q on his last diamond and retains four clubs in dummy. East cannot keep four clubs and also the ♡ K.

which follow, a hundred more difficult hands await the reader. If he switched to a heart—or to any other suit—in this last Quiz in PART ONE, he can expect to return high scores in PARTS TWO and THREE.

Part Two

Greek Chorus

The quizzes to come differ in two respects from those which have preceded them. They are more difficult, some of them much more so, and marks are awarded for the correct answers.

As the reader watches and measures his progress, he must not expect too big a score. Only a player well above average can hope to reach out to 200 or so, and the author himself, though he might not admit it, would take his full share of 'wrong views' if the hands were dealt him at the table.

Our heroes, East and West, are doubtless better players than they were fifty quizzes ago, but the task awaiting them is a stern one. A hundred contracts remain to be broken and each time the dice seem loaded in declarer's favour.

FINAL REMINDER

Before turning over the page to Quiz 51, the reader is reminded of the author's challenge. He can start, if he likes, with Quiz 101 (page 218) and come back later. Though neither group of quizzes is more difficult than the other, and the same total of 350 marks is awarded for each, he cannot fail to score more for the fifty he does last. For as he turns the pages, his defence will improve and the evidence will be there to prove it. The author will say: 'I told you so,' and everyone will be happy ever after—except poor South whom nobody loves.

QUESTIONS

(51)

North deals.

South	North
—	1 ♡
1 ♠	3 ♠
3 NT	4 ♠

E/W pass throughout

What should East lead from:

(a) ♠ A 3 2
    ♡ A 10 7 6 5 3
    ♢ Q
    ♣ J 10 9

(b) ♠ A 2
    ♡ 10 7 6 5 3 2
    ♢ Q
    ♣ J 10 9 8

(52)

West deals.   E/W vulnerable.

South	West	North	East
—	1 ♡	1 ♠	Dble
2 ♢	—		

What should West lead?

(a) ♠ 10
    ♡ A J 9 6 5 2
    ♢ 7 5
    ♣ A K 8 4

(b) ♠ 10
    ♡ A J 9 6 5 2
    ♢ K J 8 3
    ♣ K 3

QUESTIONS

(53)

South deals and bids 3 NT. All pass.

(South's bid is the Acol or 'gambling' 3 NT, based on a long, solid suit with little else outside.)

What should West lead from:

(a) ♠ A Q 6
    ♡ Q J 10 9 6
    ♢ 4
    ♣ K J 4 2

(b) ♠ K J 2
    ♡ K J
    ♢ J 10 9 8
    ♣ J 10 9 8

(54)

South deals.

South	North
2 NT	3 NT

E/W pass throughout

What should West lead from:

(a) ♠ K J
    ♡ K 10 8 6 2
    ♢ A 7 2
    ♣ K J 3

(b) ♠ J 10 8
    ♡ K 6 5 4 3 2
    ♢ 7
    ♣ J 10 9

ANSWERS

(*a*) ◇ Q.   3

North must have four spades or he would have passed
3 NT. Since, however, he opened 1 ♡ he has presumably
five hearts. South's 3 NT rebid suggests no more than
four spades and at least one heart. That leaves East with
one heart or none and with two spades.

If West opens the ♡ A and gives East an immediate heart
ruff, the defence will come to three tricks. No more, for
West's only entry is the ♠ A and the trick he takes with it
will deprive East of his sole remaining trump.

The diamond lead sets the stage for the decisive trick, a
ruff *by West*. East, of course, still gets his heart ruff, but...

(*b*) ♡ 10.   3

The difference between this hand and the last is that now
West has only two trumps and East should have three. If
East has no heart at all, which is quite likely, he may get
two ruffs. And if he has the ◇ A, he will not only get two
ruffs himself, but he will give West a ruff, too.

West leads the ♡ 10, his highest, as a SUIT PREFERENCE
SIGNAL, directing East's attention to diamonds.

(52)

(*a*) ♡ A.   3

A penalty double at the one level, especially at unfavour-
able vulnerability, is usually a warning to partner which
says: 'I hate your suit.'

East, therefore, is quite likely to have a singleton heart—
or even a void—and the top clubs may serve as precious
entries for West to give his partner heart ruffs. West cannot
afford to part with one of them 'to look at the table'.

(*b*) ♠ 10.   3

East is as likely as ever to be short in hearts, but unless he
has the ♠ A, too, how is he going to put West back to
give him a second ruff? And if he has the ♠ A, the opening of the ♠ 10 will be far more effective.

Did West forget to double? Careless of him, but that's
neither here nor there.

ANSWERS

(53)

(*a*) ♠ A. 2

This isn't the right setting for suit development. Time presses, for as soon as declarer gains the lead he will reel off seven or eight tricks in diamonds.

Before committing himself, West should look at the table. Partner may encourage spades or perhaps a club switch will be indicated. There will still be time to lead a heart, should that look best.

(*b*) ♠ K. 4

Declarer is going to be unlucky. His solid suit isn't as solid as he thought. But is it clubs or diamonds? West can't tell and must leave both minors strictly alone.

Meanwhile spades hold out better prospects than hearts since West has three of them.

(54)

(*a*) A low diamond.

All partner can be expected to contribute is some desul- 2
tory jack and even that is doubtful. West should forget about him and adopt a purely passive defence, giving away as little as possible.

The ◇ 2 is 'correct', but the ◇ 7 is vaguely misleading and declarer is there to be misled. As for poor partner, he hardly comes into it.

(*b*) ♠ J. 3

This time, partner alone matters. He is marked with a few high cards and West should try to find his suit. Other things being equal, it is better to lead spades than clubs, for no trump bidders often conceal a minor, but rarely a major.

Hearts? You will hardly have time to develop so ragged a suit and you may easily present declarer with a trick he does not deserve.

QUESTIONS

(55)

North deals.

South	North
—	Pass
1 ♠	3 ♠
4 ♣	4 ♠
6 ♠	—

E/W pass throughout

What should West lead from:

(a) ♠ 7 4
    ♡ J 10 9 8
    ◇ 10 9 8
    ♣ K J 4 3

(b) ♠ 7 6 4
    ♡ J 10 9 8 6 3
    ◇ 10
    ♣ A Q 3

QUESTIONS

(56)

South deals. Both sides vulnerable.

South	West	North	East
1 ♠	Dble	Pass	Pass
Pass	—		

What should West lead from:

(a) ♠ 10 9
    ♡ A K 10 6
    ◇ K Q 10
    ♣ A J 9 7

(b) ♠ Q
    ♡ A K 10 6
    ◇ K Q 10 2
    ♣ A J 9 7

ANSWERS

Marks

(a) ♣ 3.   4

South's bidding is highly suspicious. Since he intended to bid the slam, anyway, even though North had no feature to show and signed off hard, what was the purpose of the alleged cue bid of 4 ♣? Was he contemplating a grand slam? Most unlikely. A far more probable explanation is that he hoped to inhibit a club lead, and what better reason could West have for making one?

(b) ♣ A.   4

The same reason applies as in (a) above. The singleton diamond would be a particularly bad lead, for if partner has the ◇ A—or a trump trick—the contract will be beaten anyway.

The other two hands are probably something like:

DECLARER:	DUMMY:
♠ A J 9 8 5 3	♠ K Q 10 2
♡ A	♡ K Q 7 2
◇ A K J 3	◇ Q 4 2
♣ 10 5	♣ 8 7

ANSWERS

Marks

(*a*) ♠ 10.   2

(*b*) ♠ Q.   3

By leaving in West's take-out double East shows length in trumps and the defence should, therefore, concentrate on cutting down declarer's ruffing value, not only in dummy, but above all in his own hand. His trumps may be something like: A K 7 6 5 or A J 7 3 2. He must make his tops, but he may be prevented from taking tricks with his low trumps—if trumps are attacked at once.

The defence should, in short, pursue the reverse of a 'forcing game' and restrict declarer's opportunities of forcing himself.

There is no basic difference between (*a*) and (*b*). It goes against the grain to lead a singleton trump, but declarer does it often enough when he has a singleton in dummy. The position here is not dissimilar, for spades have been chosen as the trump suit by East no less than by South.

(57)

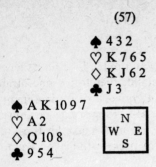

```
        ♠ 4 3 2
        ♡ K 7 6 5
        ◇ K J 6 2
        ♣ J 3
♠ A K 10 9 7    ┌─────┐
♡ A 2           │  N  │
◇ Q 10 8        │W   E│
♣ 9 5 4         │  S  │
                └─────┘
```

Neither side vulnerable
Dealer: South

South	West	North	East
1 ♡	1 ♠	2 ♡	2 ♠
3 ♡	Pass	Pass	3 ♠
Pass	Pass	4 ♡	

CONTRACT: 4 ♡.

West opens with three rounds of spades.

Declarer ruffs the third spade, lays down the ♣ A and ♣ K and ruffs a club in dummy. Returning to his hand with the ◇ A, he leads another club.

Which card should West play?

QUESTIONS

(58)

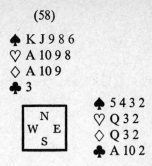

♠ K J 9 8 6
♡ A 10 9 8
◇ A 10 9
♣ 3

♠ 5 4 3 2
♡ Q 3 2
◇ Q 3 2
♣ A 10 2

Both sides vulnerable
Dealer: South

South	North
1 NT	2 ♣ (STAYMAN)
2 ♠	6 ♠

E/W pass throughout

CONTRACT: 6 ♠.

West leads the ♣ K.
Which card should East play?

ANSWERS

Marks
10

♡ A.

Declarer can have no losers in the side suits, so the only hope for the defence is to score two trump tricks. This is impossible unless East has the ♡ Q and even then the odds are tilted in declarer's favour. On the bidding, he will not fail to place West with the ♡ A, and the ♡ Q will fall tamely on the king—or crash with the ace on the second round.

Note that ruffing with the ace can cost nothing wherever the ♡ Q may be.

Maybe South didn't play too well. All the more reason for not letting him get away with it.

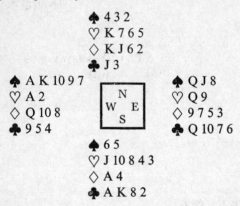

```
              ♠ 4 3 2
              ♡ K 7 6 5
              ◇ K J 6 2
              ♣ J 3
♠ A K 10 9 7            ♠ Q J 8
♡ A 2          N        ♡ Q 9
◇ Q 10 8    W     E     ◇ 9 7 5 3
♣ 9 5 4         S       ♣ Q 10 7 6
              ♠ 6 5
              ♡ J 10 8 4 3
              ◇ A 4
              ♣ A K 8 2
```

ANSWERS

(58)

♣ A.   5

West can't have a trump and a switch by him to either red suit would probably help declarer. What's more, he might see the ♣ 10 or the deuce as SUIT PREFERENCE SIGNALS. Maybe he wouldn't, but East shouldn't take a needless risk. Overtaking the ♣ K he leads a trump, leaving declarer to do his own work.

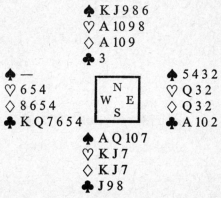

```
                    ♠ K J 9 8 6
                    ♡ A 10 9 8
                    ◇ A 10 9
                    ♣ 3
    ♠ —                              ♠ 5 4 3 2
    ♡ 6 5 4          N               ♡ Q 3 2
    ◇ 8 6 5 4      W   E             ◇ Q 3 2
    ♣ K Q 7 6 5 4    S               ♣ A 10 2
                    ♠ A Q 10 7
                    ♡ K J 7
                    ◇ K J 7
                    ♣ J 9 8
```

QUESTIONS

(59)

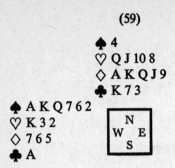

♠ 4
♡ Q J 10 8
◇ A K Q J 9
♣ K 7 3

♠ A K Q 7 6 2
♡ K 3 2
◇ 7 6 5
♣ A

```
      N
   W     E
      S
```

E/W vulnerable
Dealer: West

South	West	North	East
—	1 ♠	Dble	2 ♠
4 ♡			

CONTRACT: 4 ♡.

West leads the ♣ A.
Which card should West lead at trick two?

QUESTIONS

(60)

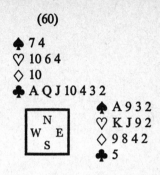

♠ 7 4
♡ 10 6 4
♢ 10
♣ A Q J 10 4 3 2

♠ A 9 3 2
♡ K J 9 2
♢ 9 8 4 2
♣ 5

Both sides vulnerable
Dealer: South

South	North
1 NT	3 NT
(16–18)	

E/W pass throughout

CONTRACT: 3 NT.

West leads the ♠ 5.
East plays the ♠ A and declarer the ♠ 8.
Which card should East lead at trick two?

(59) *Marks*

♠ 2. 5

West can take three tricks for the defence, but it's obvious from the bidding that East can contribute nothing. The only hope of beating the contract lies in a club ruff, yet that, in turn, requires an entry to East's hand.

Can there be an entry in a trickless hand? Yes. East *may* have the ♠ J. It isn't even unlikely and it is the only real hope of defeating 4 ♡.

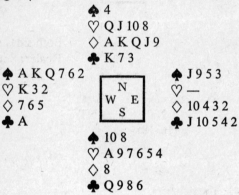

```
                    ♠ 4
                    ♡ Q J 10 8
                    ◇ A K Q J 9
                    ♣ K 7 3
  ♠ A K Q 7 6 2                    ♠ J 9 5 3
  ♡ K 3 2          N              ♡ —
  ◇ 7 6 5        W   E            ◇ 10 4 3 2
  ♣ A              S              ♣ J 10 5 4 2
                    ♠ 10 8
                    ♡ A 9 7 6 5 4
                    ◇ 8
                    ♣ Q 9 8 6
```

ANSWERS

♡ J.   5

East knows that West has no more than four spades, for the
♠ 5 was led and he can see the four, three and two. So even if
South has no guard in spades he will make his contract, unless
West can produce an ace quickly. And if West can do that,
the contract may be defeated even if South has a spade
stopper.

Hoping to find partner with the ♡ A, East plays the ♡ J
through the closed hand. If declarer covers with the queen,
West wins and leads a heart through dummy's 10 6 up to
East's K 9 2. If declarer ducks, East continues with a low
heart and picks up the ♡ Q on the next round.

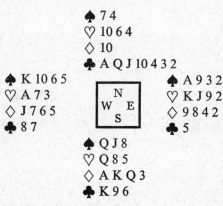

```
                    ♠ 7 4
                    ♡ 10 6 4
                    ◇ 10
                    ♣ A Q J 10 4 3 2
    ♠ K 10 6 5          ┌─────┐          ♠ A 9 3 2
    ♡ A 7 3             │  N  │          ♡ K J 9 2
    ◇ J 7 6 5          W│     │E         ◇ 9 8 4 2
    ♣ 8 7               │  S  │          ♣ 5
                        └─────┘
                    ♠ Q J 8
                    ♡ Q 8 5
                    ◇ A K Q 3
                    ♣ K 9 6
```

QUESTIONS

(61)

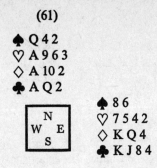

♠ Q 4 2
♡ A 9 6 3
◇ A 10 2
♣ A Q 2

```
        N
    W       E
        S
```

♠ 8 6
♡ 7 5 4 2
◇ K Q 4
♣ K J 8 4

N/S vulnerable
Dealer: North

South	North
—	1 NT
4 ♠	—

E/W pass throughout

CONTRACT: 4 ♠.

West leads the ♡ K.

Declarer goes up with the ♡ A, ruffs a heart, crosses to dummy with the ♠ Q and ruffs another heart. After drawing a second round of trumps—West following—declarer goes over to the table with the ◇ A and leads dummy's last heart.

Which should be East's remaining seven cards?

QUESTIONS

(62)

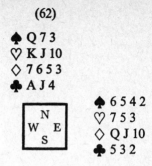

♠ Q 7 3
♡ K J 10
◇ 7 6 5 3
♣ A J 4

♠ 6 5 4 2
♡ 7 5 3
◇ Q J 10
♣ 5 3 2

E/W vulnerable
Dealer: North

South	West	North	East
		Pass	Pass
1 ♡	2 ♠	4 ♡	Pass
6 ♡			

CONTRACT: 6 ♡.

West leads the ♠ K.

Declarer ruffs and draws three rounds of trumps, West discarding two spades and a club. Next come the ◇ A, the ◇ K and a third diamond on which West throws another black card.

What card should East lead when he comes in (trick seven) with the ◇ Q?

ANSWERS

Marks

$\heartsuit$ 7 $\diamondsuit$ Q (or K) 4 $\clubsuit$ K J 8 4   5

Unless East has retained the $\diamondsuit$ 4, all is lost. After ruffing the last heart, declarer will play a diamond and East will have to lead a club into dummy's A Q 2.

Declarer doesn't know, of course, the exact position, but the club finesse can't run away and meanwhile he is giving himself the added chance of an end-play. His persistence in eliminating hearts should alert East to the danger—and to the urgency of keeping an *exit card*.

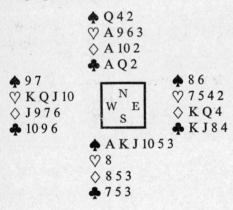

```
              ♠ Q 4 2
              ♡ A 9 6 3
              ◇ A 10 2
              ♣ A Q 2
  ♠ 9 7                      ♠ 8 6
  ♡ K Q J 10      N          ♡ 7 5 4 2
  ◇ J 9 7 6     W   E        ◇ K Q 4
  ♣ 10 9 6        S          ♣ K J 8 4
              ♠ A K J 10 5 3
              ♡ 8
              ◇ 8 5 3
              ♣ 7 5 3
```

ANSWERS

A club.   10

East can count South's hand for seven hearts, four diamonds, and therefore, two clubs. If he has the ♣ Q, the contract is unbeatable for the finesse is right. So East must
assume that his partner has both the ♣ K and ♣ Q.

If, after coming in with the ◇ Q, he leads a spade, declarer
will ruff, and play off all his winners. When the last red card
hits the table, West will be left with: ♠ A and ♣ K Q.
Dummy will have the ♠ Q and the ♣ A J, and West will
have to play before dummy.

To break up the squeeze, East should attack at once declarer's vital link with dummy—the ♣ A.

How can East foresee the squeeze in time? By counting.
He can identify ten winners for declarer in trumps and diamonds. The ♣ A will be the eleventh. The twelfth can only
materialize through a squeeze in the black suits.

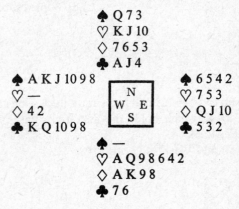

$$
\begin{array}{c}
\spadesuit\ Q\ 7\ 3 \\
\heartsuit\ K\ J\ 10 \\
\diamondsuit\ 7\ 6\ 5\ 3 \\
\clubsuit\ A\ J\ 4
\end{array}
$$

Hand layout:

Dummy (North):
- ♠ Q 7 3
- ♡ K J 10
- ◇ 7 6 5 3
- ♣ A J 4

West:
- ♠ A K J 10 9 8
- ♡ —
- ◇ 4 2
- ♣ K Q 10 9 8

East:
- ♠ 6 5 4 2
- ♡ 7 5 3
- ◇ Q J 10
- ♣ 5 3 2

South:
- ♠ —
- ♡ A Q 9 8 6 4 2
- ◇ A K 9 8
- ♣ 7 6

QUESTIONS

(63)

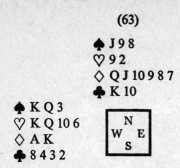

♠ J 9 8
♡ 9 2
◇ Q J 10 9 8 7
♣ K 10

♠ K Q 3
♡ K Q 10 6
◇ A K
♣ 8 4 3 2

```
   N
W     E
   S
```

Both sides vulnerable
Dealer: South

South	*North*
1 NT (16–18)	3 NT

E/W pass throughout

CONTRACT: 3 NT.

West, who showed commendable restraint in passing through-out, leads the ♡ K which holds the first trick. East plays the ♡ 5 and declarer the ♡ 4.

Which card should West lead at trick two?

(64)

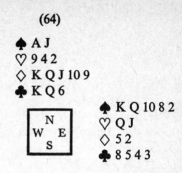

♠ A J
♡ 9 4 2
◇ K Q J 10 9
♣ K Q 6

♠ K Q 10 8 2
♡ Q J
◇ 5 2
♣ 8 5 4 3

Neither side vulnerable
Dealer: South

South	*North*
Pass	1 ◇
1 NT	2 NT
3 NT	

E/W pass throughout

CONTRACT: 3 NT.

West leads the ♡ 7.

East's ♡ J is taken by declarer's ♡ K and three rounds of
diamonds follow, the ◇ K, ◇ Q and ◇ J. The ◇ A has not yet
appeared.

Which card should East play on the third round of diamonds?

(63)

♠ 3.

It is apparent to West, that though South must have the minimum 16 for his 1 NT, East can hardly have a single point. He may, however, just have the ♠ 10 and that should be enough to beat the contract. With nothing to guide him—how wise West was not to bid or double!—declarer has no reason to go up with dummy's ♠ J. He will doubtless play the nine. East's ten will drive out the ace and West will have two spades to cash in good time.

The full deal could be:

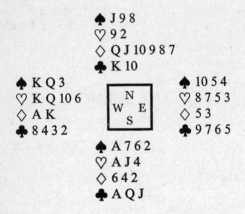

```
                    ♠ J 9 8
                    ♡ 9 2
                    ♢ Q J 10 9 8 7
                    ♣ K 10
  ♠ K Q 3                              ♠ 10 5 4
  ♡ K Q 10 6          N                ♡ 8 7 5 3
  ♢ A K           W       E            ♢ 5 3
  ♣ 8 4 3 2           S                ♣ 9 7 6 5
                    ♠ A 7 6 2
                    ♡ A J 4
                    ♢ 6 4 2
                    ♣ A Q J
```

ANSWERS

Marks

♡ Q.

5

Apply the Rule of Eleven. West led the ♡ 7, so he must have all but four cards (11−7=4) higher than the 7. East had two, one is in dummy and the king has been played. West must, therefore, have the ♡ A 10 8, but he may be afraid to play a heart in case declarer started with ♡ K Q x. East should clear up the position at once by discarding his queen.

West must have either the ◇ A or the ♣ A. If it is the ◇ A, which seems likely, he must take his hearts at once. Otherwise declarer will reel off nine tricks with: one heart, four diamonds, three (or four) clubs and the ♠ A.

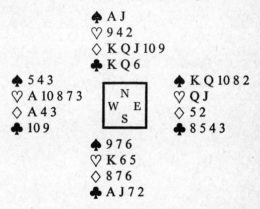

```
                    ♠ A J
                    ♡ 9 4 2
                    ◇ K Q J 10 9
                    ♣ K Q 6
      ♠ 5 4 3                        ♠ K Q 10 8 2
      ♡ A 10 8 7 3      N            ♡ Q J
      ◇ A 4 3       W       E        ◇ 5 2
      ♣ 10 9           S            ♣ 8 5 4 3
                    ♠ 9 7 6
                    ♡ K 6 5
                    ◇ 8 7 6
                    ♣ A J 7 2
```

QUESTIONS

(65)

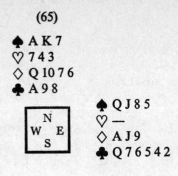

♠ A K 7
♡ 7 4 3
◇ Q 10 7 6
♣ A 9 8

♠ Q J 8 5
♡ —
◇ A J 9
♣ Q 7 6 5 4 2

Rubber Bridge
E/W vulnerable and 30
Dealer: South

South	North
Pass	1 NT (12–14)
3 ♡	

E/W pass throughout

CONTRACT: 3 ♡.

West leads the ♠ 9.

Winning with dummy's ♠ K, declarer plays a trump to his ♡ Q, then a club to the ace and another club which he ruffs with the ♡ 8 in his hand.

Crossing to the table with the ♠ A, he ruffs dummy's last club with the ♡ 9 and exits with the ♠ 10. West follows and East wins.

What card should East play (trick eight)?

QUESTIONS

(66)

♠ 4 3 2
♡ 3 2
◇ Q 4
♣ A K Q 10 6 3

```
        N
    W       E
        S
```

♠ 9 8 6 5
♡ 7 4
◇ A 3 2
♣ 9 8 5 4

Neither side vulnerable
Dealer: South

South	North
1 ♡	2 ♣
2 ♠	3 ♣
3 NT	

E/W pass throughout

CONTRACT: **3 NT.**

West leads the ◇ 5.
Declarer plays the ◇ 4 from dummy.
(a) Which card should East play?
(b) What is the suit pattern of declarer's hand?

(65)

$\diamondsuit$ 9.

Marks

8

By now East should know all about South's hand. His trumps must be: A K Q 10 9 8. Since he ruffed with the $\heartsuit$ 8 and the $\heartsuit$ 9, he must surely have the ten. East can see all the remaining black cards and this leaves South with three small diamonds. He cannot have the $\diamondsuit$ K—or seven hearts—for he passed as dealer.

Having reduced his trumps twice, declarer now has the same number as West and his best hope is that in the three-card ending the lead will run up to his $\heartsuit$ A K 10.

To prevent this happening, defenders must take their diamonds at once, making sure that East should be on play at the critical moment—when declarer and West have only trumps left—to lead *through* the closed hand. West will then score his $\heartsuit$ J for the fifth trick to break the contract.

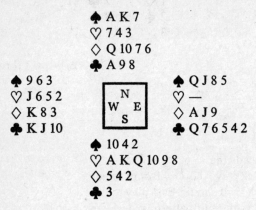

ANSWERS

(66)

Marks

(*a*) ◇ 3 or ◇ 2. 2
(*b*) 4–5–4–0. 3

Since the ◇ 5 was led and the three cards below it are on view, West cannot have more than four diamonds. That means that South, too, must have four diamonds. His reverse bidding sequence showed nine cards in the majors, so he cannot have a club.

Should East go up with the ◇ A, dummy's ◇ Q may provide an entry to six otherwise inaccessible clubs.

You don't like the bidding? Neither do I, but that is the worst of all reasons for allowing South to make his contract.

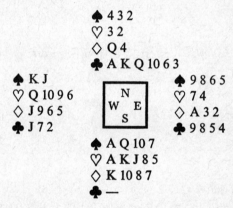

♠ 4 3 2
♡ 3 2
◇ Q 4
♣ A K Q 10 6 3

♠ K J
♡ Q 10 9 6
◇ J 9 6 5
♣ J 7 2

♠ 9 8 6 5
♡ 7 4
◇ A 3 2
♣ 9 8 5 4

♠ A Q 10 7
♡ A K J 8 5
◇ K 10 8 7
♣ —

QUESTIONS

(67)

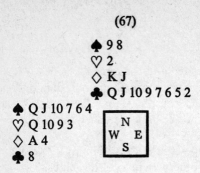

♠ 9 8
♡ 2
♢ K J
♣ Q J 10 9 7 6 5 2

♠ Q J 10 7 6 4
♡ Q 10 9 3
♢ A 4
♣ 8

TEAMS OF FOUR
E/W vulnerable
Dealer: West

South	West	North	East
—	2 ♠*	3 ♣	Pass
3 NT			

CONTRACT: 3 NT.

West leads the ♠ Q.
East wins with the ♠ A and returns the deuce on which declarer plays the ♠ K.
Which card should West play?

(68)

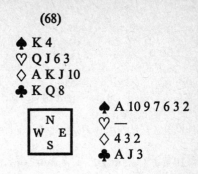

♠ K 4
♡ Q J 6 3
◇ A K J 10
♣ K Q 8

♠ A 10 9 7 6 3 2
♡ —
◇ 4 3 2
♣ A J 3

E/W vulnerable
Dealer: East

South	West	North	East
—	—	—	1 ♠
Pass	2 ♠	Dble	3 ♠
4 ♡			

CONTRACT: 4 ♡.

West leads the ♠ Q.
The ♠ K is played from dummy and East wins.
Which card should East lead at trick two?

ANSWERS

♠ 10.   10

Did you fail to get this right? Then you are in good company. One of America's leading pairs had their wires crossed in this situation during a friendly international. West played the ♠ 7, a middle card designed to show that his entry was in the middle suit, diamonds.

East argued, correctly, that since West was marked on the lead with the ♠ J 10, the jack would signal hearts and the 10 would call for a diamond. The four, of course, would be the suit signal for clubs.

West, a world champion, had overlooked the fact that he might have had no ace at all. That was what the ♠ 7, an essentially neutral card, suggested to East. When he came in with the ♣ A, he returned a heart and. . . .

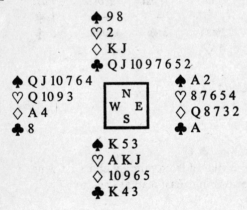

```
                    ♠ 9 8
                    ♡ 2
                    ◇ K J
                    ♣ Q J 10 9 7 6 5 2
    ♠ Q J 10 7 6 4        ┌─────┐        ♠ A 2
    ♡ Q 10 9 3            │  N  │        ♡ 8 7 6 5 4
    ◇ A 4                 │W   E│        ◇ Q 8 7 3 2
    ♣ 8                   │  S  │        ♣ A
                          └─────┘
                    ♠ K 5 3
                    ♡ A K J
                    ◇ 10 9 6 5
                    ♣ K 4 3
```

(68)

♣ 3.

East can see that there is no hope of breaking the contract unless West produces the ♡ A or ♡ K. He is quite likely to have one or other (what other high card can he have?), but that still comes to no more than three tricks for the defence. Can East find a fourth? Maybe, if West has the ♣ 10. At trick two that ten will drive out one of dummy's honours and when West comes in with his presumed trump trick, he will lead another club through dummy's ♣ K (Q) x.

East must attack clubs at once, before declarer draws trumps and sets about the diamonds. Needless to say declarer cannot have a second spade.

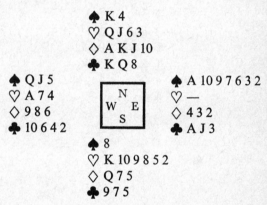

```
              ♠ K 4
              ♡ Q J 6 3
              ◇ A K J 10
              ♣ K Q 8
  ♠ Q J 5           ┌─────┐    ♠ A 10 9 7 6 3 2
  ♡ A 7 4           │  N  │    ♡ —
  ◇ 9 8 6         W │     │ E  ◇ 4 3 2
  ♣ 10 6 4 2        │  S  │    ♣ A J 3
                    └─────┘
              ♠ 8
              ♡ K 10 9 8 5 2
              ◇ Q 7 5
              ♣ 9 7 5
```

QUESTIONS

(69)

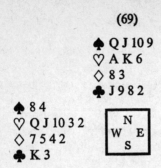

♠ Q J 10 9
♡ A K 6
◇ 8 3
♣ J 9 8 2

♠ 8 4
♡ Q J 10 3 2
◇ 7 5 4 2
♣ K 3

Neither side vulnerable
Dealer: North

South	North
—	Pass
1 ♠	3 ♠
4 ◇	4 ♡
6 ♠	

E/W pass throughout

CONTRACT: 6 ♠.

West leads the ♡ Q.

Declarer wins with the ♡ K, draws trumps—East following twice—and goes on to eliminate the red suits; the ◇ A K and a diamond ruff in dummy, then the ♡ A and a heart ruff in the closed hand. Next he plays the ♣ A.

Can declarer make his contract against good defence? If not, which East-West cards will take tricks?

(70)

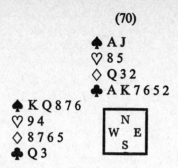

```
        ♠ A J
        ♡ 8 5
        ◇ Q 3 2
        ♣ A K 7 6 5 2
♠ K Q 8 7 6      ┌─────────┐
♡ 9 4            │    N    │
◇ 8 7 6 5        │  W   E  │
♣ Q 3            │    S    │
                 └─────────┘
```

N/S vulnerable
Dealer: South

South	West	North	East
Pass	Pass	1 ♣	1 ♡
1 ♠	Pass	2 ♣	Pass
2 NT	Pass	3 NT	

CONTRACT: 3 NT.

West leads the ♡ 9.
East overtakes with the ♡ 10 and continues with the ♡ K and ♡ Q.
Declarer wins the third trick with the ♡ A.
Which card should West play?

(69)   *Marks*

Declarer should lose tricks to East's ♣ Q and ♣ 10.   5

If declarer had another diamond he would have ruffed it. So West can count his hand for five trumps, two hearts, and three diamonds, leaving him with ♣ A x x. If he had the ♣ 10 (or ♣ Q) he couldn't lose. He would lead the ♣ 9 from dummy and run it, and even if West had both the ♣ K and ♣ Q, it wouldn't help him for he would be end-played.

It follows that declarer has two small clubs and will lose both—though only if West knows what is happening and throws his king of clubs under the ace. Otherwise he will be forced to win the next (tenth) trick and concede a ruff and discard.

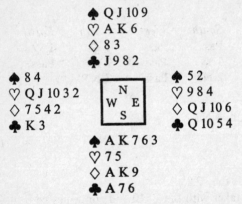

```
                    ♠ Q J 10 9
                    ♡ A K 6
                    ◇ 8 3
                    ♣ J 9 8 2
    ♠ 8 4                            ♠ 5 2
    ♡ Q J 10 3 2       N            ♡ 9 8 4
    ◇ 7 5 4 2      W       E        ◇ Q J 10 6
    ♣ K 3              S            ♣ Q 10 5 4
                    ♠ A K 7 6 3
                    ♡ 7 5
                    ◇ A K 9
                    ♣ A 7 6
```

ANSWERS

♣ Q.

West should have a pretty good picture of South's hand. To make up the values for his 2 NT bid South must have the ◇ A K, since he has the only 4 points in hearts and none in spades. East's only possible entry, then, can be the ♣ J, and the ♣ Q threatens to rob him of it. West must cast her away quickly.

See what happens if he doesn't. Declarer leads a club to the ♣ A at trick four, gets back to his hand with a diamond, leads another club—and ducks promptly when he sees West's queen. Now East's ♣ J ceases to be an entry.

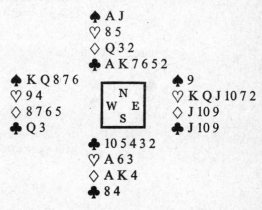

```
                    ♠ A J
                    ♡ 8 5
                    ◇ Q 3 2
                    ♣ A K 7 6 5 2
   ♠ K Q 8 7 6                      ♠ 9
   ♡ 9 4            ┌───────┐       ♡ K Q J 10 7 2
   ◇ 8 7 6 5        │   N   │       ◇ J 10 9
   ♣ Q 3           W│       │E      ♣ J 10 9
                    │   S   │
                    └───────┘
                    ♣ 10 5 4 3 2
                    ♡ A 6 3
                    ◇ A K 4
                    ♣ 8 4
```

QUESTIONS

(71)

♠ Q 10 9 8 2
♡ A Q 10 4
◇ 2
♣ 4 3 2

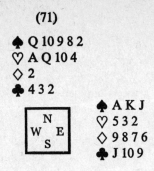

♠ A K J
♡ 5 3 2
◇ 9 8 7 6
♣ J 10 9

Neither side vulnerable
Dealer: South

South	North
1 ◇	1 ♠
2 ♣	2 ♡
2 NT	3 ♠
3 NT	

E/W pass throughout

CONTRACT: 3 NT.

West leads the ◇ Q which holds.

West continues with the ◇ J. Winning with the ◇ K, declarer leads the ♠ 7. West follows with the ♠ 3 and the deuce is played from dummy.

Which tricks does East hope to make and in which order does he hope to make them?

(72)

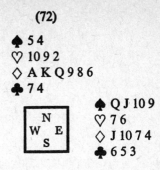

♠ 5 4
♡ 10 9 2
♢ A K Q 9 8 6
♣ 7 4

♠ Q J 10 9
♡ 7 6
♢ J 10 7 4
♣ 6 5 3

Neither side vulnerable
Dealer: South

South	North
2 ♣	3 ♢
3 ♠	4 ♢
4 ♡	5 ♢
6 NT	

E/W pass throughout

CONTRACT: 6 NT.

West leads the ♣ Q.
Declarer wins with the ♣ K and leads the ♠ 3.
West follows with the deuce and East wins.
Which card should East lead at trick three?

(71)

Marks

♠ A; ♠ J; ♠ K; another diamond.

5

Declarer is evidently hoping to make three tricks in spades, which he can do if West has the jack, a 50–50 chance. Should East win the first spade with jack, however, he will see that this plan won't work and he will be forced to try the hearts, and East knows—though declarer doesn't—that the hearts will be kind to him.

To encourage him to persist with spades, East wins the first trick with the ♠ A (or K) and continues diamonds, setting up his ◇ 9. Then he waits patiently for the next spade—to his jack.

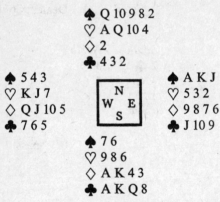

ANSWERS

◇ J (or 10).   8

Why the little spade? If declarer is looking for a safety play, why doesn't he duck a diamond? Then, even against a 4–1 break, he could make sure of five winners. He can hardly hope for better things in spades.

The most likely reason for declarer's play is that he hasn't got two diamonds. Yet he must have one, for with a void he surely wouldn't have jumped to 6 NT.

Now the picture comes into focus. Declarer isn't trying to establish anything, but to set the stage for a squeeze—to RECTIFY THE COUNT—by giving up an inevitable loser. Clearly the squeeze will be in diamonds and spades, and East should break it up by leading a diamond, so as to cut declarer's communications with dummy—in good time.

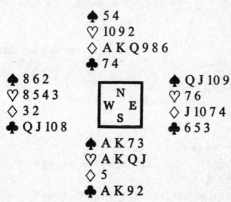

Observe what happens if East does not lead a diamond to trick three. Come down to four cards. Dummy will have all diamonds. Declarer, when he plays his last winner, a heart or the ♣ A, will have: ♠ 7 ♡ — ◇ 5 ♣ 9 2. And East?

QUESTIONS

(73)

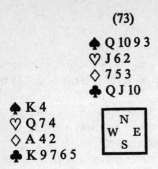

♠ Q 10 9 3
♡ J 6 2
◇ 7 5 3
♣ Q J 10

♠ K 4
♡ Q 7 4
◇ A 4 2
♣ K 9 7 6 5

```
  N
W   E
  S
```

Neither side vulnerable
Dealer: South

South	North
2 NT	3 NT

E/W pass throughout

CONTRACT: 3 NT.

West leads the ♣ 6.

Dummy's ♣ Q wins, East following with the deuce and declarer with the ♣ 3.

At trick two declarer leads the ♠ Q and runs it to West's ♠ K. What card should West lead at trick three?

QUESTIONS

(74)

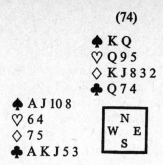

♠ K Q
♡ Q 9 5
◇ K J 8 3 2
♣ Q 7 4

♠ A J 10 8
♡ 6 4
◇ 7 5
♣ A K J 5 3

E/W vulnerable
Dealer: North

South	*North*
—	1 NT (12–14)
6 ♡	

E/W pass throughout

CONTRACT: 6 ♡.

West leads the ♣ K.
East plays the ♣ 6 and declarer the ♣ 10.
Which card should West play at trick two?

ANSWERS

Marks
5

A club.

West can account for all the high cards—21–22 with South, 6 in dummy and 12 in his own hand, leaving a jack at most for East. But though East may hold a Yarborough, he can have three little clubs. If so, declarer started with a doubleton and his ace will now come down. That is West's only hope and he should be quick to seize it, before declarer drives out the ◇ A and gathers nine tricks.

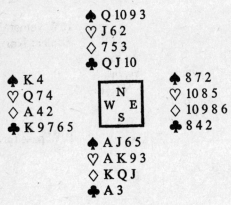

```
              ♠ Q 10 9 3
              ♡ J 6 2
              ◇ 7 5 3
              ♣ Q J 10
  ♠ K 4                        ♠ 8 7 2
  ♡ Q 7 4        N             ♡ 10 8 5
  ◇ A 4 2     W     E          ◇ 10 9 8 6
  ♣ K 9 7 6 5    S             ♣ 8 4 2
              ♠ A J 6 5
              ♡ A K 9 3
              ◇ K Q J
              ♣ A 3
```

ANSWERS

♣ A.   5

The ♣ 2 is missing and that points the way. Yet at rubber bridge, misunderstandings must be taken into account and East's ♣ 6 is not altogether conclusive. Is it the lowest of three or has he the ♣ 2 as well, and is trying to show four clubs? Or maybe East and West have no clear-cut understanding on what to do in this particular situation and there is room for doubt. West need not try too hard to interpret that ♣ 6, for there is a valuable clue in the bidding.

If South had losers in two suits he would have surely invoked the Blackwood or Gerber conventions to check on aces. The fact that he jumped straight to 6 ♡ points strongly to a void somewhere.

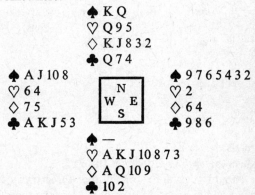

QUESTIONS

(75)

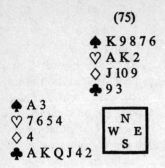

♠ K 9 8 7 6
♡ A K 2
◇ J 10 9
♣ 9 3

♠ A 3
♡ 7 6 5 4
◇ 4
♣ A K Q J 4 2

E/W vulnerable
Dealer: North

South	West	North	East
—	—	Pass	Pass
1 ♠	3 ♣	4 ♠	

CONTRACT: 4 ♠.

West leads the ♣ K.

East plays the ♣ 6 and declarer the ♣ 5.

Where should West look for another three tricks to beat the contract? In which order does he hope to make them?

QUESTIONS

(76)

♠ Q 7 4
♡ A 6 5
◇ 9
♣ A K Q J 10 8

```
      N
   W     E
      S
```

♠ K 10 9 2
♡ 4 3
◇ A 8 7 6 3
♣ 9 5

Neither side vulnerable
Dealer: South

South	North
1 ♡	3 ♣
3 ♡	4 ♡
4 NT	6 ♣
6 ♡	

E/W pass throughout

CONTRACT: 6 ♡.

West leads the ♠ A.
What card should East play?

ANSWERS

(75)

Marks 5

♠ A; ♣ 10; ♠ 3—a diamond ruff.

At trick two, after the ♣ K, West leads his singleton diamond. Then, when he comes in with the ♠ A, he underleads his top clubs, hoping to find East with the ♣ 10 and to get a diamond ruff.

This defence will succeed only some of the time, but no other offers much hope, for South is marked with the ◇ A on the bidding and if he is missing the king, the finesse will succeed.

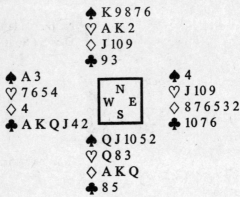

```
                    ♠ K 9 8 7 6
                    ♡ A K 2
                    ◇ J 10 9
                    ♣ 9 3
  ♠ A 3                              ♠ 4
  ♡ 7 6 5 4          N              ♡ J 10 9
  ◇ 4             W     E           ◇ 8 7 6 5 3 2
  ♣ A K Q J 4 2      S              ♣ 10 7 6
                    ♠ Q J 10 5 2
                    ♡ Q 8 3
                    ◇ A K Q
                    ♣ 8 5
```

ANSWERS

Marks

♠ K.

10

Does East want another spade or a diamond?

A moment's reflection will tell him that declarer can hardly have a void since he applied Blackwood. Therefore East wants a diamond switch and the one and only way to ensure it is by dropping the ♠ K!

Declarer would not have bid as he did with a topless spade suit. So East's ♠ K cannot be a singleton. But with the king gone, dummy's queen is the master card, so West has no choice but to switch.

It is true that North should not have responded 6 ♣, but 5 ♡, which South would have passed. Not visualizing an aceless hand opposite, he made a dubious bid and should have paid the penalty—which he didn't when the hand was played at Crockford's Club in London.

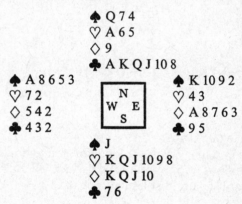

```
              ♠ Q 7 4
              ♡ A 6 5
              ◇ 9
              ♣ A K Q J 10 8
♠ A 8 6 5 3        N         ♠ K 10 9 2
♡ 7 2          W     E       ♡ 4 3
◇ 5 4 2            S         ◇ A 8 7 6 3
♣ 4 3 2                      ♣ 9 5
              ♠ J
              ♡ K Q J 10 9 8
              ◇ K Q J 10
              ♣ 7 6
```

(77)

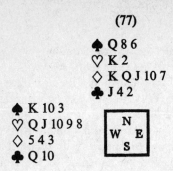

♠ Q 8 6
♡ K 2
◊ K Q J 10 7
♣ J 4 2

♠ K 10 3
♡ Q J 10 9 8
◊ 5 4 3
♣ Q 10

```
    N
 W     E
    S
```

Neither side vulnerable
Dealer: South

South	North
1 NT	3 NT
(12–14)	

E/W pass throughout

CONTRACT: 3 NT.

West leads the ♡ Q.

Winning in dummy with the king declarer continues with the
♠ 6. East follows with the deuce and the jack falls to West's king.
Which card should West lead at trick three?

(78)

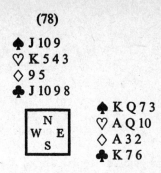

♠ J 10 9
♡ K 5 4 3
◇ 9 5
♣ J 10 9 8

♠ K Q 7 3
♡ A Q 10
◇ A 3 2
♣ K 7 6

N
W E
S

Both sides **vulnerable**
Dealer: East

South	West	North	East
—	—	—	1 ♠
2 ◇			

CONTRACT: 2 ◇.

West led the ♠ A, then the ♠ 2.

East won with the ♠ Q, declarer following with the ♠ 4 and ♠ 5.

Defenders made four more tricks to break the contract.

Which tricks did they make and in which order did they make them?

ANSWERS

♣ Q.

West should be able to place every card that matters.

Trick one showed that declarer has the ♡ A. He must have the ◇ A, too. Otherwise he would have first attended to his long suit. The play to trick two indicates that his spades are headed by the A J and that he is setting up his ninth trick, to add to the other eight—five diamonds, two hearts and the ♠ A.

Declarer's high card strength already comes to 13, only one point short of the maximum for a non-vulnerable 1 NT. He cannot, therefore, have another king and it follows that East must have both the ace and king of clubs. An immediate switch to the ♣ Q should give the defence a fine chance of beating the contract. But there's not a moment to lose, for declarer now has his nine tricks.

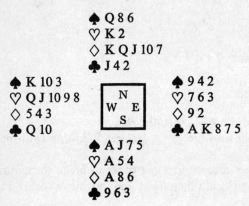

```
            ♠ Q 8 6
            ♡ K 2
            ◇ K Q J 10 7
            ♣ J 4 2
♠ K 10 3        ┌─────┐        ♠ 9 4 2
♡ Q J 10 9 8    │  N  │        ♡ 7 6 3
◇ 5 4 3         │W   E│        ◇ 9 2
♣ Q 10          │  S  │        ♣ A K 8 7 5
                └─────┘
            ♠ A J 7 5
            ♡ A 5 4
            ◇ A 8 6
            ♣ 9 6 3
```

ANSWERS

Marks

A low spade ruffed by West; the two red aces and the ♠ K.   8

The key to the correct defence was to lead a low spade, not the king, at trick three.

Had East led the ♠ K, declarer would have lived to score the ♠ 8 or else he would have ruffed it in dummy. As it was, East, at trick three, led a small spade for West to ruff. He came in with a heart, led the ace and another trump, and later made the ♠ K.

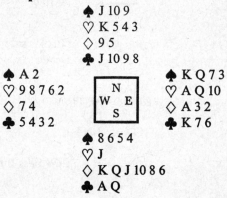

```
                    ♠ J 10 9
                    ♡ K 5 4 3
                    ◇ 9 5
                    ♣ J 10 9 8
    ♠ A 2                           ♠ K Q 7 3
    ♡ 9 8 7 6 2       N             ♡ A Q 10
    ◇ 7 4         W       E         ◇ A 3 2
    ♣ 5 4 3 2         S             ♣ K 7 6
                    ♠ 8 6 5 4
                    ♡ J
                    ◇ K Q J 10 8 6
                    ♣ A Q
```

(79)

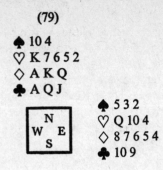

♠ 10 4
♡ K 7 6 5 2
◇ A K Q
♣ A Q J

♠ 5 3 2
♡ Q 10 4
◇ 8 7 6 5 4
♣ 10 9

Neither side vulnerable
Dealer: North

South	North
—	1 ♡
1 NT	3 NT

E/W pass throughout

CONTRACT: 3 NT.

West leads the ♠ Q.

Declarer wins with the ace, plays a club to dummy's jack and continues at trick three with the ♡ 2.

Which tricks will East-West make and in which order will they make them?

QUESTIONS

(80)

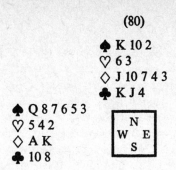

♠ K 10 2
♡ 6 3
◇ J 10 7 4 3
♣ K J 4

♠ Q 8 7 6 5 3
♡ 5 4 2
◇ A K
♣ 10 8

```
   N
 W   E
   S
```

Neither side vulnerable
Dealer: South

South	*North*
1 ◇	2 ◇
2 NT	3 NT

CONTRACT: 3 NT.

West led the ♠ 6.
Declarer played low from dummy and went up with the ♠ A on East's ♠ 9.
At trick two West came in with the ◇ K.
The contract was defeated.
What was the defence?

ANSWERS

           Marks

♡ Q, ♡ A and three spades.   8

The opening lead pinpoints the ♠ A K with declarer. The
♠ A at trick one was not a clever card to play, but that's not
East's concern. What matters is that since South responded a
modest 1 NT to 1 ♡, he cannot have another ace. So West
has the ♡ A—and he will need it badly as an entry to the
spades. To preserve that entry East should go up fearlessly
with his ♡ Q to lead a spade while he has the chance.

Observe what happens if East plays low. West wins with
the ♡ A and leads a spade, which holds. Declarer wins the
next spade, repeats the club finesse and clears the hearts. East
still makes his ♡ Q but, alas, he has no more spades and
West has no more entries.

East can expect to find his partner with five spades. If he
had four only, South would have four, too, and if so, his response to 1 ♡ would have doubtless been 1 ♠, not 1 NT.

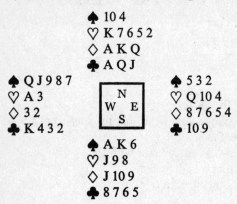

                   ♠ 10 4
                   ♡ K 7 6 5 2
                   ◇ A K Q
                   ♣ A Q J

♠ Q J 9 8 7   ♠ 5 3 2
♡ A 3   **N**   ♡ Q 10 4
◇ 3 2   **W**   **E**   ◇ 8 7 6 5 4
♣ K 4 3 2   **S**   ♣ 10 9

                   ♠ A K 6
                   ♡ J 9 8
                   ◇ J 10 9
                   ♣ 8 7 6 5

Marks

At trick three West returned the ♠ Q.   10

On his 2 NT rebid South was marked with at least A J x in hearts, so spades alone held out any hope for the defence.

The play at trick one showed that East had started with ♠ J 9 and South—who surely wouldn't have bid 2 NT with a bare ♠ A—with ♠ A 4. West could see that if, at trick three, he led a low spade, declarer would insert dummy's ♠ 10 and lose to East's ♠ J. Alas, East would have no spade left to return.

This was clear to West, but South couldn't tell how the spades were divided. By leading the ♠ Q West made it look as if he had the ♠ J as well. Hoping that the ◇ A would be with East, South naturally held up dummy's ♠ K. West could now clear his suit.

(81)

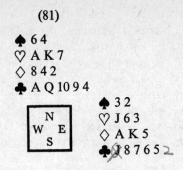

♠ 6 4
♡ A K 7
◇ 8 4 2
♣ A Q 10 9 4

♠ 3 2
♡ J 6 3
◇ A K 5
♣ J 8 7 6 5 2

Both sides vulnerable
Dealer: South

South	North
1 ♠	2 ♣
4 ♠	

E/W pass throughout

CONTRACT: 4 ♠.

West leads the ◇ Q.
Which four tricks does East hope to make to defeat the contract and in which order does he hope to make them?

(82)

♠ Q J 10
♡ A 7
◇ 10 5
♣ A Q J 9 8 4

♠ K 8 6
♡ Q J 10 9 8
◇ A Q 3
♣ K 10

```
    N
W       E
    S
```

Neither side vulnerable
Dealer: North

South	West	North	East
—	—	1 ♣	Pass
1 ◇	1 ♡	2 ♣	Pass
3 ◇	Pass	3 ♡	Pass
3 NT			

CONTRACT: 3 NT.

West leads the ♡ Q.

Declarer goes up with dummy's ♡ A, East following with the deuce, and runs the ◇ 10.

Which tricks does West hope to make and in which order does he hope to make them?

(81)   *Marks*

◇ K; a club ruffed by West; ◇ A; a second club ruffed by   8
West.

East's first reaction on seeing dummy must be one of sur-
prise that North made no effort to reach a slam.

Paradoxically, that reflection should lead East to find the best
defence against a mere game. He will ask himself: where
could South find the values for so strong a rebid? A good fit
for partner's clubs must be the answer and if it's as good as
K J 3—which isn't asking too much—West must have a void.
So East overtakes the ◇ Q and leads a club for West to ruff.
Then the process is repeated.

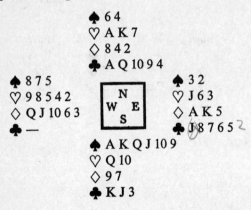

```
                    ♠ 6 4
                    ♡ A K 7
                    ◇ 8 4 2
                    ♣ A Q 10 9 4
   ♠ 8 7 5              N          ♠ 3 2
   ♡ 9 8 5 4 2      W       E      ♡ J 6 3
   ◇ Q J 10 6 3         S          ◇ A K 5
   ♣ —                             ♣ J 8 7 6 5
                    ♠ A K Q J 10 9
                    ♡ Q 10
                    ◇ 9 7
                    ♣ K J 3
```

ANSWERS

(82) *Marks*

♢ A; ♢ Q; three hearts.   10

South's bidding suggests a six-card diamond suit and his
line of play bears this out. He attacks diamonds first, hoping
to find East with the ♢ Q. That should give him nine tricks
with five diamonds, two hearts, one club and one spade
(♠ A).

He wouldn't have called 3 NT without a spade guard and
the play to the first trick confirms the ♡ K.

Should West win the first diamond with the queen, declarer
will have to abandon diamonds and go for the clubs—and
six tricks will fall into his lap.

To encourage a diamond continuation, West should take
the ♢ 10 with the ♢ A, clear his hearts and sit back. Declarer will surely cross to dummy with the ♣ A—dismissing
West's ♣ 10 with a contemptuous look—and repeat the
'marked' diamond finesse. At that point Nemesis will overtake him.

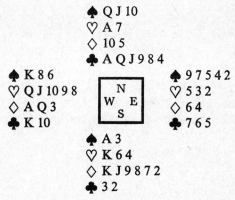

        ♠ Q J 10
        ♡ A 7
        ♢ 10 5
        ♣ A Q J 9 8 4

♠ K 8 6   ♠ 9 7 5 4 2
♡ Q J 10 9 8   N   ♡ 5 3 2
♢ A Q 3   W E   ♢ 6 4
♣ K 10   S   ♣ 7 6 5

        ♠ A 3
        ♡ K 6 4
        ♢ K J 9 8 7 2
        ♣ 3 2

(83)

♠ J 10 7 3
♡ A K Q J
♢ 10
♣ A Q 10 6

```
        N
    W       E
        S
```

♠ K Q 2
♡ 7 5 3 2
♢ A J 5 2
♣ J 2

N/S vulnerable
Dealer: West

South	West	North	East
—	3 ♢	Dble*	5 ♢
5 ♠			

CONTRACT: 5 ♠.

West leads the ♢ K.

(a) Which card should East play?

(b) Which card should East play when he gains the lead?

QUESTIONS

(84)

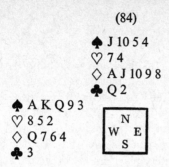

♠ J 10 5 4
♡ 7 4
◇ A J 10 9 8
♣ Q 2

♠ A K Q 9 3
♡ 8 5 2
◇ Q 7 6 4
♣ 3

N
W E
S

N/S vulnerable
Dealer: South

South	West	North	East
2 ♡	2 ♠	3 ◇	Pass
4 ♣	Pass	4 ♡	Pass
5 ♣	Pass	5 ◇	Pass
6 ♡			

CONTRACT: 6 ♡.

West leads the ♠ K.
East follows with the deuce and declarer with the ♠ 6.
What should West play at trick two?

ANSWERS

Marks

(*a*) ◇ A.   2

(*b*) A club (preferably, the jack).   6

How can East make both his ♠ K and ♠ Q? Only by per-suading declarer that he is threatened by an imminent ruff. Overtaking the ◇ K with the ◇ A, East should lead a club. It's a luxury he can well afford, for declarer can have no losers in the side suits, but the impression is created that East has a singleton and will ruff the next club. To stop him, declarer may forego the safety play and lay down the ace of trumps.

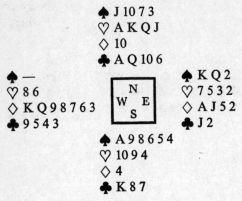

```
                    ♠ J 10 7 3
                    ♡ A K Q J
                    ◇ 10
                    ♣ A Q 10 6
  ♠ —                              ♠ K Q 2
  ♡ 8 6              N             ♡ 7 5 3 2
  ◇ K Q 9 8 7 6 3  W   E          ◇ A J 5 2
  ♣ 9 5 4 3          S             ♣ J 2
                    ♠ A 9 8 6 5 4
                    ♡ 10 9 4
                    ◇ 4
                    ♣ K 8 7
```

ANSWERS

A diamond.

Marks
10

Prospects are bleak. Declarer's trumps must be solid and he has advertised a good five-card club suit as well. West's singleton club is the only ray of sunshine. Maybe partner can be awkward, as in the diagram below.

But what will happen if West leads another spade—or a trump or his singleton club?

Declarer will ruff and reel off his winners, probably six hearts and four good-looking clubs. Coming down to two cards and discarding before dummy, West will have to keep the best spade. So he will have to bare his ◇ Q.

What about East? If, as West hopes, he has the master club, he, too, will be left with one diamond and all dummy's diamonds will be good.

By switching to a diamond at trick two, West disrupts declarer's communications with dummy and breaks up the threat of a double squeeze.

```
                ♠ J 10 5 4
                ♡ 7 4
                ◇ A J 10 9 8
                ♣ Q 2
  ♠ A K Q 9 3    ┌─────────┐    ♠ 8 7 2
  ♡ 8 5 2        │    N    │    ♡ 6 3
  ◇ Q 7 6 4      │  W   E  │    ◇ K 5 3
  ♣ 3            │    S    │    ♣ 10 9 6 5 4
                └─────────┘
                ♠ 6
                ♡ A K Q J 10 9
                ◇ 2
                ♣ A K J 8 7
```

(85)

♠ A K J 9
♡ 3 2
◇ A 5 4
♣ A K 8 7

	♠ Q 10 7 6
	♡ 9 4
	◇ 6 3 2
	♣ Q J 10 9

```
    N
W       E
    S
```

Neither side vulnerable
Dealer: East.

South	West	North	East
—	—	—	Pass
Pass	1 ♡	Dble	Pass
2 ◇	Pass	3 ◇	Pass
4 ◇	Pass	5 ◇	Pass

CONTRACT: 5 ◇.

West leads the three top hearts.
Declarer ruffs the third heart with dummy's ◇ A.
Which card should East play?

QUESTIONS

(86)

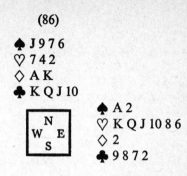

♠ J 9 7 6
♡ 7 4 2
◇ A K
♣ K Q J 10

♠ A 2
♡ K Q J 10 8 6
◇ 2
♣ 9 8 7 2

Neither side vulnerable
Dealer: North

South	West	North	East
—	—	1 ♣	1 ♡
1 ♠	2 ♡	2 ♠	Pass
4 ♠			

CONTRACT: 4 ♠.

West leads the ♣ A.
Which card should East play?

ANSWERS

A trump.   10

If declarer has a trump loser he will go down anyway and
if he has six good diamonds, he has eleven top tricks. East
must assume, therefore, that declarer has five diamonds only
and therefore a doubleton in at least one of the black suits. If
East discards from that suit, a ruff will set up the long card
to give declarer the extra trick he needs.

Under-ruffing, though always spectacular, cannot cost a
trick in this situation—and as may be seen from the diagram
below, it is the only way of breaking the contract.

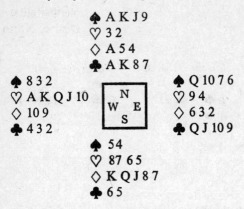

ANSWERS

Marks

♣ 2.

5

It is obvious that East's ♣ A is a singleton. Left to himself, West will try to put East in with a heart, since he bid the suit, but though he will still get his club ruff—when East comes in with the ♠ A—it will not be enough to break the contract.

Wanting not a heart, but a diamond, East follows to the ♣ A with the deuce. West, who is looking for guidance, will see it as a SUIT PREFERENCE SIGNAL, calling for a diamond. He will lead one at trick two—and another for East to ruff, when he himself ruffs a club.

If West has a third trump, as in the diagram, declarer will go two down instead of making his contract.

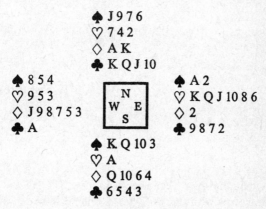

```
              ♠ J 9 7 6
              ♡ 7 4 2
              ◇ A K
              ♣ K Q J 10
♠ 8 5 4                        ♠ A 2
♡ 9 5 3          N             ♡ K Q J 10 8 6
◇ J 9 8 7 5 3  W   E           ◇ 2
♣ A              S             ♣ 9 8 7 2
              ♠ K Q 10 3
              ♡ A
              ◇ Q 10 6 4
              ♣ 6 5 4 3
```

QUESTIONS

(87)

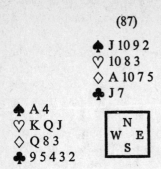

♠ J 10 9 2
♡ 10 8 3
◇ A 10 7 5
♣ J 7

♠ A 4
♡ K Q J
◇ Q 8 3
♣ 9 5 4 3 2

Neither side vulnerable
Dealer: South

South	North
1 ♠	2 ♠
4 ♠.	

E/W pass throughout

CONTRACT: 4 ♠.

West leads the ♠ A, then the ♠ 4.

Declarer wins with the ♠ Q, takes one more round of trumps, to which East follows, and cashes the ♣ A and ♣ K.

Next he plays the ♡ A and exits with the seven to West's Queen. East plays the ♡ 4, then the deuce.

West continues with the ♡ K to which all follow.

Eight cards have been played: three trumps, two clubs and three hearts.

What should West lead at trick nine?

QUESTIONS

(88)

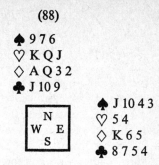

♠ 9 7 6
♡ K Q J
◇ A Q 3 2
♣ J 10 9

♠ J 10 4 3
♡ 5 4
◇ K 6 5
♣ 8 7 5 4

E/W vulnerable
Dealer: South

South	*North*
1 ♡	2 ◇
2 ♡	4 ♡

E/W pass throughout

CONTRACT: 4 ♡.

West leads out the three top clubs.

Declarer ruffs the third time and draws three rounds of trumps, West following and East shedding the ◇ 5.

The three top spades come next.

On the third spade West discards the ♣ 2.

With nine cards gone declarer leads his last trump. Dummy's last three cards are: ◇ A Q 3.

What should be East's last three cards?

ANSWERS

(87)

A club.   5

No doubt this will present declarer with a ruff and discard, but will it do him any good?

Count his hand. He had four trumps, since East followed three times. With a third club he would have doubtless ruffed it in dummy. What of the hearts? East followed with the ♡ 4 before the deuce, showing an even number. It must be four, not two, for he has produced three already. That means that declarer had three hearts and therefore four diamonds, the same 4–3–4–2 pattern as dummy.

If he now ruffs a club in one hand and discards a diamond from the other, he will still lose a diamond. He probably won't—playing for split honours—if West leads a diamond.

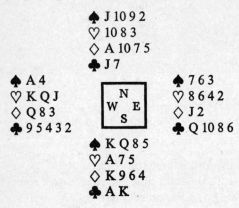

```
                    ♠ J 10 9 2
                    ♡ 10 8 3
                    ◇ A 10 7 5
                    ♣ J 7
  ♠ A 4                              ♠ 7 6 3
  ♡ K Q J          N                 ♡ 8 6 4 2
  ◇ Q 8 3        W   E               ◇ J 2
  ♣ 9 5 4 3 2       S                ♣ Q 10 8 6
                    ♠ K Q 8 5
                    ♡ A 7 5
                    ◇ K 9 6 4
                    ♣ A K
```

ANSWERS

♠ J   ◇ K   ♣ any   5

It is very worrying for East, but declarer knows too much about his hand. West has shown up already with the ♣ A K Q and is unlikely to have the ◇ K as well. East is known to have the ♠ J and declarer will be sorely tempted to throw him in with it, so as to make him lead into dummy's ◇ A Q. If East hasn't left himself with a club, he will be helpless. But, of course, he anticipated the end-play, kept a little club, unknown to declarer, and bared his ◇ K—all with effortless ease.

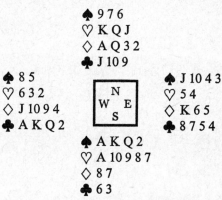

```
              ♠ 9 7 6
              ♡ K Q J
              ◇ A Q 3 2
              ♣ J 10 9
♠ 8 5                          ♠ J 10 4 3
♡ 6 3 2        N               ♡ 5 4
◇ J 10 9 4   W   E             ◇ K 6 5
♣ A K Q 2      S               ♣ 8 7 5 4
              ♠ A K Q 2
              ♡ A 10 9 8 7
              ◇ 8 7
              ♣ 6 3
```

QUESTIONS

(89)

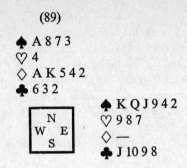

♠ A 8 7 3
♡ 4
♢ A K 5 4 2
♣ 6 3 2

♠ K Q J 9 4 2
♡ 9 8 7
♢ —
♣ J 10 9 8

N/S vulnerable
Dealer: West

South	*West*	*North*	*East*
—	3 ♢	Pass	Pass
4 ♡			

CONTRACT: 4 ♡.

West leads the ♢ Q.
Declarer plays dummy's deuce.
Which card should East play?

QUESTIONS

(90)

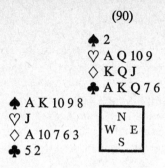

♠ 2
♡ A Q 10 9
◇ K Q J
♣ A K Q 7 6

♠ A K 10 9 8
♡ J
◇ A 10 7 6 3
♣ 5 2

N
W E
S

Both sides vulnerable
Dealer: South

South	West	North	East
Pass	1 ♠	Dble	Pass
2 ♡	Pass	4 ♡	

CONTRACT: 4 ♡.

West leads the ♠ K.
East follows with the ♠ 6 and declarer with the ♠ 5.
What card should West lead at trick two?

(89)

A trump.

Why did declarer play low? Clearly because he expected East to have a void. An opening Three-Bid is usually made on a seven-card suit and declarer probably has a singleton. If so, defenders must knock out dummy's ♠ A quickly, before trumps are drawn and the two top diamonds come into their own. Of course, West can see that as well as East, but what if he has no spade? It isn't so very unlikely and there is no need for East to run the risk. He should ruff and lead his ♠ K like a man.

Now it will be up to West—not to ruff! If he does, he will undo all East's good work and South will make eleven tricks instead of nine.

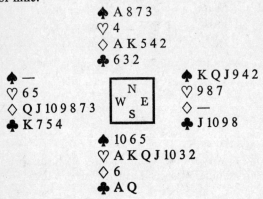

```
                    ♠ A 8 7 3
                    ♡ 4
                    ◇ A K 5 4 2
                    ♣ 6 3 2
    ♠ —                           ♠ K Q J 9 4 2
    ♡ 6 5            N             ♡ 9 8 7
    ◇ Q J 10 9 8 7 3  W   E        ◇ —
    ♣ K 7 5 4           S          ♣ J 10 9 8
                    ♠ 10 6 5
                    ♡ A K Q J 10 3 2
                    ◇ 6
                    ♣ A Q
```

ANSWERS

A low diamond.   5

West can see two tricks only for the defence, his two aces. Partner may have the ♡ K, but that still isn't enough to beat the contract, unless he can also ruff something. He is unlikely to have a singleton anywhere, for with a singleton, the ♡ K and even a minor fit in spades—his ♠ 6 suggests four spades or the queen or both—he might have found a raise to 2 ♠ over North's double. So West should play him for a doubleton diamond.

A low diamond keeps open the lines of communication and leaves West with the ◇ A as a vital entry to the third diamond, the one East will ruff.

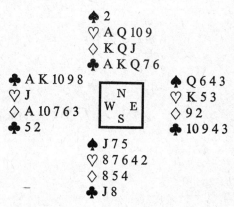

QUESTIONS

(91)

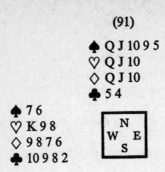

```
                    ♠ Q J 10 9 5
                    ♡ Q J 10
                    ♢ Q J 10
                    ♣ 5 4
    ♠ 7 6              ┌─────────┐
    ♡ K 9 8           │    N    │
    ♢ 9 8 7 6         │ W     E │
    ♣ 10 9 8 2        │    S    │
                       └─────────┘
```

Neither side vulnerable
Dealer: South

South	North
2 ♣	2 NT
3 ♣	3 ♠
4 NT	5 ♣
5 NT	6 ♣

E/W pass throughout

CONTRACT: 6 ♣.

West leads the ♣ 10.

East throws the ♡ 3. Declarer wins with the ♣ A and continues with the ♣ K and ♣ Q.

In which order should West follow?

(92)

♠ J 8 3
♡ 5 4 3
◇ K Q J
♣ A Q 10 9

```
      N
   W     E
      S
```

♠ A Q 9 4 2
♡ 9 8 2
◇ A 10 2
♣ K 5

E/W vulnerable
Dealer: East

South	West	North	East
—	—	—	1 ♠
Pass	Pass	Dble	Pass
2 ♡			

CONTRACT: 2 ♡.

West leads the ♠ 6.
East covers dummy's eight with the nine.
Declarer wins with the ♠ 10 and leads a diamond.
If the contract is defeated, which will be the first four tricks lost by declarer and in which order will he lose them?

Marks
10

♣ 8 and ♣ 9—or vice versa.

The bidding points to the correct defence. South must have all four aces, but only two kings. Otherwise he would have twelve top tricks. East must, therefore, have one king. With A x x in any side suit, declarer would give up a trick in that suit and gain access to dummy, finding there his twelfth trick.

West must, therefore, defend on the assumption that declarer's pattern is 2–2–2–7—A K in one side suit, A x in the two others. Even so, declarer can make his contract—on a guess. After drawing trumps and cashing his A K (spades in the diagram below), he leads his ace and other heart. No matter what West returns, declarer is in dummy and his troubles are over.

But unless West looks a couple of moves ahead, declarer can eliminate all guesswork and make certain of his contract by throwing West in with his fourth trump. After winning a trump trick to which he is not entitled, West will present declarer with two others which destiny hadn't allotted to him.

To avoid this end-play, West should retain to the end his ♣ 2.

Look at it this way. If West parts with his ♣ 2—the natural thing to do—declarer *may* present him with a trump trick, if it suits him. The choice will lie with declarer. So long as West retains the deuce, declarer will have no choice.

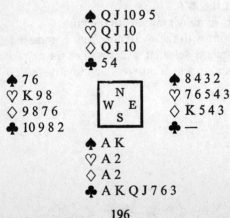

```
              ♠ Q J 10 9 5
              ♡ Q J 10
              ◇ Q J 10
              ♣ 5 4
♠ 76                          ♠ 8 4 3 2
♡ K 9 8      N               ♡ 7 6 5 4 3
◇ 9 8 7 6  W   E             ◇ K 5 4 3
♣ 10 9 8 2     S             ♣ —
              ♠ A K
              ♡ A 2
              ◇ A 2
              ♣ A K Q J 7 6 3
```

ANSWERS

Marks

The ♡ K (or ♡ Q); the ♠ A; a spade ruff; the ◇ A.　8

This is a problem in communications. To keep the lines open, East ducks *twice*, once in spades and once in diamonds.

Declarer is evidently going to take a finesse in trumps and on the bidding partner is quite likely to have a trump trick.

East counts. He can see five tricks—his two aces, partner's presumed trump trick, a spade ruff and the ♣ K. It's not enough. Can another trick be conjured up somewhere? Maybe if West's trumps are as good as K 10 x or even Q 10 x. He can then ruff two spades, so long as he can put East in twice. Hence the virtue of holding up the ◇ A—the entry to the *second* spade ruff. By then, it is true, declarer, having no more spades himself, will be able to ruff high. But then East's ♡ 9 may be promoted unexpectedly into a full-blown trick as in this diagram:

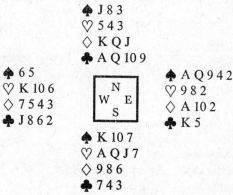

```
              ♠ J 8 3
              ♡ 5 4 3
              ◇ K Q J
              ♣ A Q 10 9
 ♠ 6 5                          ♠ A Q 9 4 2
 ♡ K 10 6        N              ♡ 9 8 2
 ◇ 7 5 4 3     W   E            ◇ A 10 2
 ♣ J 8 6 2       S              ♣ K 5
              ♠ K 10 7
              ♡ A Q J 7
              ◇ 9 8 6
              ♣ 7 4 3
```

197

QUESTIONS

(93)

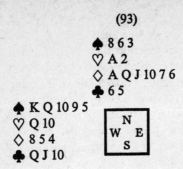

♠ 8 6 3
♡ A 2
◇ A Q J 10 7 6
♣ 6 5

♠ K Q 10 9 5
♡ Q 10
◇ 8 5 4
♣ Q J 10

| N |
| W E |
| S |

Neither side vulnerable
Dealer: South

South	*North*
1 ♣	1 ◇
2 ♣	3 ◇
3 NT	

E/W pass throughout

CONTRACT: 3 NT.

West leads the ♠ K.
East plays the ♠ 4 and declarer the ♠ J.
Which card should West lead at trick two?

QUESTIONS

(94)

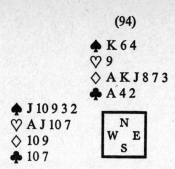

♠ K 6 4
♡ 9
♦ A K J 8 7 3
♣ A 4 2

♠ J 10 9 3 2
♡ A J 10 7
♦ 10 9
♣ 10 7

Neither side vulnerable
Dealer: South

South	*North*
1 NT	3 NT
(12–14)	

E/W pass throughout

CONTRACT: 3 NT.

West led the ♠ J.

Declarer played the ♠ 4 from dummy. East won with ♠ A and led the ♡ Q on which declarer played the ♡ 3.

To beat the contract East had to have a certain card.

(*a*) Which card was it?

(*b*) Which cards did West play to the winning tricks for his side and in which order did he play them?

(93)   *Marks*
♡ Q.   10

What are declarer's spades? A J bare? On the face of it,
there can be no other possibility. Yet if South has A J alone,
East started with ♠ 7 4 2, and if so, he wouldn't have played
the ♠ 4 on the king.

What, then, is it all about?

Understandably, South dared not win the first spade, in
case the diamond finesse failed. But why didn't he play the
♠ 2? Because he knew that West, rightly suspecting a Bath
Coup, would switch and that, evidently, was something
South was anxious to avoid. He badly wanted a second spade
from West. Then, if East came in with the ◇ K, he would
either have no spade left to play or else the suit would have
broken harmlessly. Either way it wouldn't matter.

That is what declarer must have been thinking when he
played that ♠ J. If West can work this out, and it calls for a
lot of imagination, the rest is easy. The only suit South can
fear is hearts, so West switches at trick two to the ♡ Q.

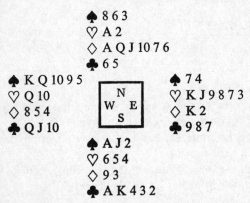

```
              ♠ 8 6 3
              ♡ A 2
              ◇ A Q J 10 7 6
              ♣ 6 5
♠ K Q 10 9 5        ┌─────┐        ♠ 7 4
♡ Q 10             │  N  │        ♡ K J 9 8 7 3
◇ 8 5 4          W │     │ E     ◇ K 2
♣ Q J 10           │  S  │        ♣ 9 8 7
                    └─────┘
              ♠ A J 2
              ♡ 6 5 4
              ◇ 9 3
              ♣ A K 4 3 2
```

Declarer's unusual play is based on a famous hand described
in *Win at Bridge with Jacoby & Son*.

ANSWERS

(94)   *Marks*

(*a*) ♡ 8.   5

(*b*) ♡ 10; ♡ 7; ♡ J; ♡ A.   5

East cannot have the ◇ Q, for only 13 points are hidden from view and declarer must have them all for his 1 NT. The only hope for defenders is to take four heart tricks and for this East must have the ♡ 8.

On the ♡ Q West unblocks, retaining the ♡ 7. This allows East to remain on play with the ♡ 8 so as to lead a third heart through the closed hand, if declarer does not cover.

If, on East's ♡ Q, West fails to unblock with the ♡ 10 (or J), he will be obliged to win the second heart trick and declarer's K x will then stop the suit.

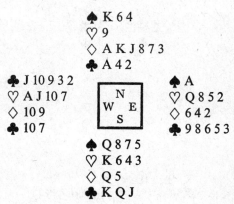

♠ K 6 4
♡ 9
◇ A K J 8 7 3
♣ A 4 2

♣ J 10 9 3 2   ♠ A
♡ A J 10 7   ♡ Q 8 5 2
◇ 10 9   ◇ 6 4 2
♣ 10 7   ♣ 9 8 6 5 3

♠ Q 8 7 5
♡ K 6 4 3
◇ Q 5
♣ K Q J

QUESTIONS

(95)

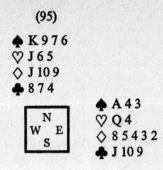

♠ K 9 7 6
♡ J 6 5
◇ J 10 9
♣ 8 7 4

♠ A 4 3
♡ Q 4
◇ 8 5 4 3 2
♣ J 10 9

Neither side vulnerable
Dealer: South

South	North
2 NT	3 ♣ (Stayman)
3 ♠	4 ♠

E/W pass throughout

CONTRACT: 4 ♠.

West led the ◇ K, then the ◇ A.

Declarer followed with the ◇ 6 and the ◇ Q.

At trick three West switched to the ♡ 9. Dummy's jack, East's queen and the ♡ K in the closed hand made up the trick.

Declarer now led the ♠ 5 to dummy's king, West following with the deuce.

The contract went one down.

Which tricks did defenders take and in which order did they take them?

(96)

♠ Q J 7 6
♡ J 4
◇ 6 4 3
♣ J 10 5 2

♠ K
♡ A K Q 10 8 6
◇ A 5
♣ Q 8 7 4

```
    N
  W   E
    S
```

Neither side vulnerable
Dealer: South

South	West	North	East
1 ♠	2 ♡	2 ♠	Pass
4 ♠			

CONTRACT: 4 ♠.

West leads the ♡ K, then the ♡ A.

East follows with the deuce and the three, and declarer with the seven and nine.

What card should West lead at trick three?

ANSWERS

Marks
5

♠ J and the ♠ A.

East could see 19 points. He had 7, dummy 5 and West had shown another 7 (◇ A K). So he knew that even if the opening 2 NT was shaded to 20, at most one jack was missing from declarer's hand and the one jack still hidden from view was the ♠ J. Hoping that West had it, East played low to the ♠ K. Declarer led a second trump and naturally inserted the ten from his hand, for of course he placed West with the ♠ A.

Had East gone up with the ♠ A the first time, declarer couldn't have gone wrong. Having no entry to dummy, he would have had no choice but to play the ♠ Q from his hand —and without malice aforethought he would have dropped West's jack.

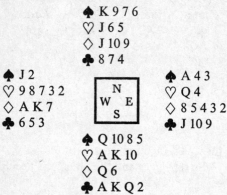

```
              ♠ K 9 7 6
              ♡ J 6 5
              ◇ J 10 9
              ♣ 8 7 4
♠ J 2                        ♠ A 4 3
♡ 9 8 7 3 2      N           ♡ Q 4
◇ A K 7       W     E        ◇ 8 5 4 3 2
♣ 6 5 3          S           ♣ J 10 9
              ♠ Q 10 8 5
              ♡ A K 10
              ◇ Q 6
              ♣ A K Q 2
```

ANSWERS

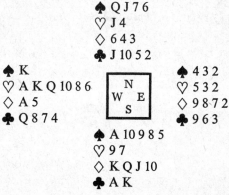

(96)

♡ Q.

Yes, it will present declarer with a ruff and discard, but it will also give him an unhoped for entry to dummy, allowing him to take the losing trump finesse—and to go one down. Without this golden opportunity he would have to play the ♠ A from his hand—and drop the singleton ♠ K.

```
                    ♠ Q J 7 6
                    ♡ J 4
                    ◇ 6 4 3
                    ♣ J 10 5 2
     ♠ K                              ♠ 4 3 2
     ♡ A K Q 10 8 6      N           ♡ 5 3 2
     ◇ A 5          W         E      ◇ 9 8 7 2
     ♣ Q 8 7 4           S           ♣ 9 6 3
                    ♠ A 10 9 8 5
                    ♡ 9 7
                    ◇ K Q J 10
                    ♣ A K
```

QUESTIONS

(97)

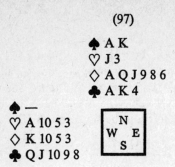

♠ A K
♡ J 3
◇ A Q J 9 8 6
♣ A K 4

♠ —
♡ A 10 5 3
◇ K 10 5 3
♣ Q J 10 9 8

E/W vulnerable
Dealer: East

South	North
3 ♠	6 ♠

E/W pass throughout

CONTRACT: 6 ♠.

West leads the ♣ Q.

All follow.

Winning in dummy with the ♣ A, declarer leads the ♠ A, on which West throws a club, then the ◇ A and a low diamond which he ruffs in his hand. Crossing to dummy with the ♣ K, he ruffs another diamond, East discarding a club.

At trick seven, declarer leads the ♡ K.

(a) Which card should West play?

(b) Which card should he play when he comes in—this trick or the next one—with the ♡ A?

QUESTIONS

(98)

```
              ♠ Q 9 4 3
              ♡ K Q 6
              ◇ J 10 9
              ♣ 8 7 6
♠ K J 2        ┌─────────┐
♡ 10 9 8       │    N    │
◇ A 5 4        │ W     E │
♣ Q 10 5 4     │    S    │
               └─────────┘
```

Neither side vulnerable
Dealer: South

South	North
1 ♡	1 ♠
2 NT	3 NT

E/W pass throughout

CONTRACT: 3 NT.

West leads the ♣ 4.
East plays the ♣ J, holds the trick and returns the ♣ 9. Declarer goes up with the ♣ A and leads a diamond to the jack, which wins.

The ◇ 10 comes next, East following with the ◇ 6, then the ◇ 7. Which card should West play when he comes in (trick four) with the ◇ A?

ANSWERS

(97)

(*a*) A low heart. 5

(*b*) Another heart. 5

Declarer has revealed his intentions. As soon as the bad trump break came to light, he began to shorten his trumps. An opening Three-Bid is usually made on a seven-card suit, so it looks as if East started with ♠ J x x x. To catch that jack declarer needs four entries in dummy—three to reduce his trumps by ruffing to East's level and one more to get to the table, so as to lead through East, after trump length has been equalized.

At trick seven, declarer has reduced his trumps by two (two diamond ruffs), but only one entry, the ♠ K, remains in dummy and he needs one more. If West goes up with the ♡ A, the ♡ J will provide that entry. So West plays low and when he wins the next heart, he is careful to play a card which declarer cannot ruff. It must be, therefore, another heart.

Note that East has shown three clubs, so South can have no more.

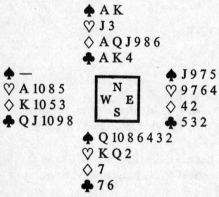

```
              ♠ A K
              ♡ J 3
              ◇ A Q J 9 8 6
              ♣ A K 4
  ♠ —                        ♠ J 9 7 5
  ♡ A 10 8 5      N          ♡ 9 7 6 4
  ◇ K 10 5 3    W   E        ◇ 4 2
  ♣ Q J 10 9 8    S          ♣ 5 3 2
              ♠ Q 10 8 6 4 3 2
              ♡ K Q 2
              ◇ 7
              ♣ 7 6
```

ANSWERS

(98)   *Marks*
                                                10

♠ J.

There can be no future in clubs for if partner had the king he would have played it. Yet unless the defence takes four more tricks quickly declarer will sail home with two clubs, three diamonds and four hearts, for he is pretty well marked with the ♡ A on the bidding. Can he have the ♠ A, too? Impossible. That would give him a 21 count and he didn't bid that way. So East has the ♠ A. He must have three others, too, for South can only have a doubleton. Why? Because he is marked with three clubs (the king by inference), four hearts at least on the bidding, and four diamonds. East, remember, followed in ascending order, showing three diamonds.

Now if East can only produce the ♠ 10 the contract can be beaten. Declarer will cover West's jack with dummy's queen and East will win with the ace. A low spade to the king will put West back in the lead and his deuce will pierce dummy's ♠ 9 4.

If the ♠ J isn't covered, West continues with the ♠ K.

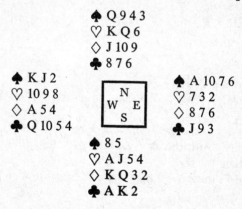

```
              ♠ Q 9 4 3
              ♡ K Q 6
              ◇ J 10 9
              ♣ 8 7 6
♠ K J 2          N         ♠ A 10 7 6
♡ 10 9 8    W       E      ♡ 7 3 2
◇ A 5 4          S         ◇ 8 7 6
♣ Q 10 5 4                 ♣ J 9 3
              ♠ 8 5
              ♡ A J 5 4
              ◇ K Q 3 2
              ♣ A K 2
```

QUESTIONS

(99)

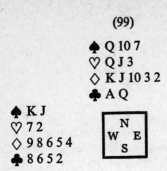

♠ Q 10 7
♡ Q J 3
◇ K J 10 3 2
♣ A Q

♠ K J
♡ 7 2
◇ 9 8 6 5 4
♣ 8 6 5 2

N
W E
S

Neither side vulnerable
Dealer: North

South	West	North	East
—	—	1 ◇	1 ♡
1 ♠	Pass	2 ♣	Pass
4 ♠			

CONTRACT: 4 ♠.

West leads the ♡ 7.

Dummy's ♡ J, East's ♡ K and declarer's ♡ 4 make up the first trick.

East switches to the ◇ Q which declarer wins with the ace.

He continues with the ♠ A and the ♠ 4, East following with the deuce, then the three.

Which card should West play when he comes in with the ♠ K?

QUESTIONS

(100)

♠ A K 3
♡ 3 2
◇ A 7 6 5
♣ K 7 6 2

♠ J 5 4
♡ J 6 5 4
◇ K 4 3
♣ Q J 10

```
┌─────┐
│  N  │
│W   E│
│  S  │
└─────┘
```

E/W vulnerable
Dealer: North

South	North
—	1 NT
	(12–14)
4 ♡	

E/W pass throughout

CONTRACT: 4 ♡.

West leads the ♣ Q.

Declarer ruffs and lays down the ♡ A on which East throws a club.

Crossing to dummy with the ♠ A, declarer ruffs a second club.

Next comes a spade to dummy's king and another club ruff; then a diamond to the ace and dummy's last club is ruffed with the ♡ K.

Eight cards have been played—the ♡ A, the ♠ A K, the ◇ A and four clubs, ruffed by declarer.

Which should be West's last five cards?

Marks
5

♡ 2.

Undoubtedly East was dealt a singleton diamond, but by following trumps naturally, in ascending order—the ♠ 2 first, then the ♠ 3—he showed that he had no more trumps. The only hope of beating the contract is, therefore, to find declarer with two more losing hearts.

Had East played the ♠ 3 before the ♠ 2, he would have shown that he had another trump and West would have returned a diamond for him to ruff.

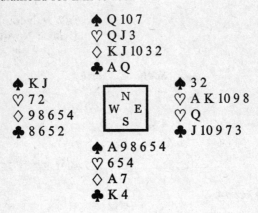

```
                    ♠ Q 10 7
                    ♡ Q J 3
                    ◇ K J 10 3 2
                    ♣ A Q
  ♠ K J                          ♠ 3 2
  ♡ 7 2           N              ♡ A K 10 9 8
  ◇ 9 8 6 5 4   W   E            ♡ Q
  ♣ 8 6 5 2       S              ♣ J 10 9 7 3
                    ♠ A 9 8 6 5 4
                    ♡ 6 5 4
                    ◇ A 7
                    ♣ K 4
```

(100)   *Marks*

♠ J; ♡ J 6; ◇ K 3.   10

That means that at trick eight (dummy's last club, ruffed
with the ♡ K) West must *under-ruff*.

By ruffing four clubs, declarer has reduced his trumps to two
—the Q 10. Unless West under-ruffs, he will be left with three
(J 6 5), one more than declarer and that is one too many, for
two tricks later, when three cards only are left, West will
have nothing but trumps. He will have to ruff something—
one of declarer's losers—and lead away from his ♡ J 6 into
the ♡ Q 10.

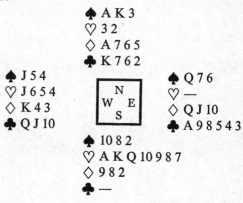

```
                    ♠ A K 3
                    ♡ 3 2
                    ◇ A 7 6 5
                    ♣ K 7 6 2
♠ J 5 4                              ♠ Q 7 6
♡ J 6 5 4        ┌─────────┐         ♡ —
◇ K 4 3          │    N    │         ◇ Q J 10
♣ Q J 10         │  W   E  │         ♣ A 9 8 5 4 3
                 │    S    │
                 └─────────┘
                    ♠ 10 8 2
                    ♡ A K Q 10 9 8 7
                    ◇ 9 8 2
                    ♣ —
```

Part Three

A Foreword

How successful were you with the last fifty quizzes? Or did you suspect a trap, and taking me at my word, you are tackling PART THREE before PART TWO? Either way, you will win, first in marks, then, when you sit down to play, in money or match points.

You will win more still if you pick up this book again in, say, six months, time. By way of an experiment you may reverse then the order in which you are now taking PARTS TWO and THREE. You will win once more, of course, but it will be instructive to see by how much. A year later you may like to come back to these quizzes a third time. Don't be afraid that you will have all the right answers. Progress is inevitable, but perfection fortunately is unattainable. So there is nothing to fear.

QUESTIONS

(101)

South deals:

South	North
1 ♠	3 ♣
4 ♣	4 ♠
4 NT	5 ◇
6 ♠	—

What should West lead from:

♠ A 2   ♡ Q 10 6 4   ◇ Q 10 6 4   ♣ 4 3 2

(102)

East deals:

South	West	North	East
—	—	—	1 ◇
2 ♠	4 ◇	4 ♠	5 ◇
5 ♠	—		

What should West lead from:

♠ 7 6 5   ♡ J 10 9 4 3   ◇ A 7 6 4 2   ♣ —

(103)

East deals:

South	West	North	East
—	—	—	1 ♡
1 ♠	2 ♡	4 ♠	—

What should West lead from:

(a) ♠ 7 5	(b) ♠ 7 5
♡ K 8 7 4 2	♡ J 10 9 8 3
◇ Q J 10	◇ Q J 10
♣ Q J 10	♣ Q J 10

QUESTIONS

(104)

South deals.

E/W pass throughout:

South	North
1 ♠	3 ♠
4 ♠	—

What should West lead from:

(a) ♠ 8 4 2   (b) ♠ K 3 2
    ♡ 2   ♡ 2
    ♢ A 7 6 4   ♢ A Q 9 4
    ♣ A 8 5 4 3   ♣ A J 9 6 3

(105)

South deals:

South	North
2 ♡	4 ♢
4 ♡	4 ♠
4 NT	5 ♡
7 ♡	—

What should West lead from:

♠ K 10 4   ♡ 9 8   ♢ 10 9 8 7 5 4   ♣ J 9

ANSWERS

(101)

Marks

♡ 4.   2

West must make an attacking lead, for once declarer has
drawn trumps, he will have one or more discards on dummy's
clubs. To which red suit should West pin his hopes? His
hearts and diamonds are identical, but while he knows nothing about East's hearts, he has noted that East didn't
double the conventional 5 ◇ response to Blackwood. With
the ◇ K, he might have done so.

Having nothing to guide him, West should make use of this
slender inference.

(102)

◇ 2.   3

This isn't going to be an easy contract to break, so it is
worth taking a risk. Partner probably has the ◇ K, and if so,
it won't take him long to realize why West underled the ace.
He will give him a club ruff, and since he opened the bidding,
maybe East can find the third, decisive trick.

(103)

(*a*) ♡ K.   2

The hearts cannot be expected to yield more than one
trick and the best chance of beating the contract lies in
finding declarer with a weak spot in one of the minors.
But which one? To gain time and information, West leads
the ♡ K, so as to be still on play at trick two to lead
through dummy's ♣ K x x—or perhaps the ◇ K x x.

(*b*) ◇ Q or the ♣ Q.   2

West is never likely to have the lead again and he should
not miss his only chance of leading through dummy. He
cannot tell which minor to attack, but either is likely to be
more vulnerable than the heart suit. To put it another
way: half a good guess is better than none.

ANSWERS

(104)

Marks

(*a*) ♣ A.   4

The first impulse is to lead the singleton, but is East likely to have an ace? If not, the heart lead will do more harm than good. Worse still, it will mean losing the initiative, the chance to look at dummy and maybe to find partner with a singleton.

This example is based on a hand from the key match between Italy and the United States in the 1968 World Olympiad. Both sides played in 4 ♠. One West led the ♣ A, found East with a singleton and beat the contract. The other West led the singleton heart—and didn't.

(*b*) A low trump.   3

Short of a miracle, partner cannot have the ♡ A, and if there is a miracle, the contract will be beaten anyway. Meanwhile, expecting nothing from partner, West should follow a passive defence and give nothing away. A heart could help declarer to develop a side-suit.

(105)

♠ K.   10

This is a Merrimac Coup at trick one. Once declarer has drawn trumps, he will have more tricks than he needs, for North's 4 ◇—a jump response to a forcing bid—promises a solid suit. But having six diamonds himself, West knows that someone must be very short of the suit. If East had a void he would have made a Lightner Double to ensure a diamond lead. If declarer has a void, he will draw trumps, cross to dummy with the ♠ A and enjoy the diamonds.

To knock out that ♠ A at once, West should not hesitate to sacrifice his king. The North-South hands may well be:

DECLARER:
♠ Q 8 3
♡ A K Q J 10 7
◇ —
♣ A K 4 2

DUMMY:
♠ A 7 2
♡ 6 4
◇ A K Q J 6 2
♣ 8 7

221

QUESTIONS

(106)

North deals. Neither side is vulnerable:

South	North
—	1 NT (12–14)
3 ♠	4 ♣
4 ◇	5 ♣
5 ♠	6 ♠

What should West lead from:

♠ 9 8   ♡ A 8 6 5 4   ◇ J 7 6   ♣ 8 4 3

QUESTIONS

(107)

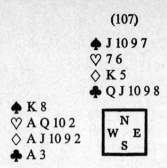

♠ J 10 9 7
♡ 7 6
◇ K 5
♣ Q J 10 9 8

♠ K 8
♡ A Q 10 2
◇ A J 10 9 2
♣ A 3

Neither side vulnerable
Dealer: South

South	West	North	East
1 ♠	Dble	3 ♠	Pass

CONTRACT: 3 ♠.

West leads the ◇ A and another diamond.

Declarer drops the ◇ Q on dummy's king and runs the jack of trumps, losing to West's king. He wins the trump return, draws another round of trumps—East follows—and continues with the ♣ K (tricks six) to West's ♣ A.

What should West play now?

ANSWERS

A low heart.   10

Underleading an ace against a slam is an unusual gambit, but a review of the bidding points to it here.

By their cue-bids in clubs and diamonds, both North and South show slam interest. Yet suddenly, despite the encouraging bid of 5 ♣, South is ready to settle for 5 ♠. Why, after so promising a start, is he giving up slam ambitions? Presumably because he has two heart losers. North gets the message, but still bids the slam. To do so he must have the second round control in hearts. It can't be a singleton, since he opened 1 NT. So it must be the ♡ K.

If West opens the ♡ A he will give the show away, and if he doesn't lead a heart at all, declarer may get rid of one. West must hope that East has the ♡ Q—but not the jack. Then his deceptive lead will surely induce declarer to misguess—and to lose an otherwise unlosable slam. The North-South hands may well be:

DECLARER: DUMMY:
♠ K Q J 7 4 3   ♠ A 10 6 2
♡ J 3   ♡ K 7
♢ A K 7   ♢ 10 9 4 2
♣ Q J   ♣ A K 4

If you conclude from the bidding that North-South are in a risky slam or if it looks as if they may have a trump loser, underleading the ♡ A is too dangerous. If they are in a good slam, as the bidding here suggests, the dangerous course may be the safest.

ANSWERS

Marks

5

♣ 3.

West should not be panicked by the sight of dummy's clubs into cashing the ♡ A and hoping to find East with the ♡ K for the setting trick.

He should count dealer's hand instead. He can pinpoint four trumps and two diamonds. Therefore if declarer has three clubs, he must have four hearts. If he has four clubs, he must have three hearts. Either way, dummy's clubs cannot provide enough discards for the hearts. West should wait patiently for the hearts to come to him.

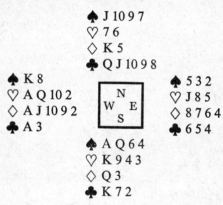

```
              ♠ J 10 9 7
              ♡ 7 6
              ◇ K 5
              ♣ Q J 10 9 8
♠ K 8                            ♠ 5 3 2
♡ A Q 10 2        N             ♡ J 8 5
◇ A J 10 9 2    W   E           ◇ 8 7 6 4
♣ A 3             S             ♣ 6 5 4
              ♠ A Q 6 4
              ♡ K 9 4 3
              ◇ Q 3
              ♣ K 7 2
```

(108)

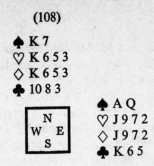

♠ K 7
♡ K 6 5 3
♢ K 6 5 3
♣ 10 8 3

                                ♠ A Q
        ┌─────────┐   ♡ J 9 7 2
        │   N   │   ♢ J 9 7 2
        │ W   E │   ♣ K 6 5
        │   S   │
        └─────────┘

Neither side vulnerable
Dealer: South

South bids 1 NT (12–14) and all pass.

CONTRACT: 1 NT.

West leads the ♠ J.
East takes the king with his ace and continues with the ♠ Q on
which West plays the ♠ 10.
Declarer's cards on the first two tricks are the ♠ 4 and ♠ 5.
What should East lead at trick three?

(109)

♠ Q 2
♡ A 2
◇ Q 10 6 5 3 2
♣ 10 8 6

```
        N
   W        E
        S
```

♠ A J 3
♡ 6 5 4 3
◇ 9 4
♣ K J 9 3

Both sides vulnerable
Dealer: South

South	North
1 NT	3 NT
(16–18)	

E/W pass throughout

CONTRACT: 3 NT.

West leads the ♡ Q.
Declarer wins with dummy's ♡ A.
Which card should East play at trick two if declarer leads:
(a) ♠ Q.
(b) ♠ 2.
(c) Which card should East play if he wins the first spade trick?

ANSWERS

♡ 2.

Marks
5

Obviously West did not start with the ♠ J 10 bare. Why, then, did he drop the ♠ 10? It was an *unnecessarily* high card, an unmistakable SUIT PREFERENCE SIGNAL, asking East to lead a heart—the highest-ranking suit—if he didn't have another spade. The ♠ 2 would have asked for a club, and the ♠ 8 (a middle card) would have suggested a diamond.

Note that only a heart return at trick three breaks the contract.

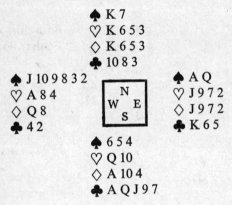

```
              ♠ K 7
              ♡ K 6 5 3
              ◇ K 6 5 3
              ♣ 10 8 3
♠ J 10 9 8 3 2        ┌───────┐        ♠ A Q
♡ A 8 4               │   N   │        ♡ J 9 7 2
◇ Q 8                 │ W   E │        ◇ J 9 7 2
♣ 4 2                 │   S   │        ♣ K 6 5
                      └───────┘
              ♠ 6 5 4
              ♡ Q 10
              ◇ A 10 4
              ♣ A Q J 9 7
```

ANSWERS

Marks

(*a*) ♠ A.   0

(*b*) ♠ A.   5

(*c*) ♣ J.   5

Obviously declarer has the ♢ A K. Otherwise he would attend to dummy's six-card suit before touching spades. On the opening lead he is marked with the ♡ K, so a spade would give him nine tricks—six diamonds, two hearts and a spade.

If declarer had the ♣ A he would have nine tricks anyway, so East should assume that West has the ♣ A. If so, and so long as it isn't a doubleton, the contract can be beaten—providing that East is wide awake at trick two. Going up with the ♠ A, he shoots the ♣ J through the closed hand. If declarer covers with the ♣ Q, West wins and returns a club through dummy's ♣ 10. If declarer plays low, East leads a second club to the ace and picks up the ten and queen on the third round.

Observe that South has enough for his 1 NT without the ♣ A.

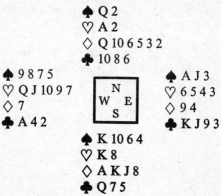

```
                    ♠ Q 2
                    ♡ A 2
                    ♢ Q 10 6 5 3 2
                    ♣ 10 8 6
  ♠ 9 8 7 5                          ♠ A J 3
  ♡ Q J 10 9 7        N             ♡ 6 5 4 3
  ♢ 7              W     E          ♢ 9 4
  ♣ A 4 2             S             ♣ K J 9 3
                    ♠ K 10 6 4
                    ♡ K 8
                    ♢ A K J 8
                    ♣ Q 7 5
```

QUESTIONS

(110)

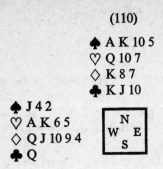

```
            ♠ A K 10 5
            ♡ Q 10 7
            ◇ K 8 7
            ♣ K J 10
♠ J 4 2          ┌─────┐
♡ A K 6 5        │   N │
◇ Q J 10 9 4     │ W   E │
♣ Q              │   S │
                 └─────┘
```

Neither side vulnerable
Dealer: South

South	*West*	*North*	*East*
Pass	1 ♡	Dble	2 ♡
2 ♠			

CONTRACT: 2 ♠.

West leads the ♣ Q, finds East with the ♣ A and ruffs a club.
Which card should West lead at trick three?

QUESTIONS

(111)

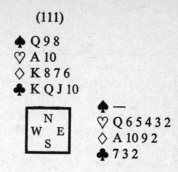

♠ Q 9 8
♡ A 10
♢ K 8 7 6
♣ K Q J 10

```
      N
   W     E
      S
```

♠ —
♡ Q 6 5 4 3 2
♢ A 10 9 2
♣ 7 3 2

Neither side vulnerable
Dealer: West

South	West	North	East
—	1 NT	Dble	2 ♡
3 ♠	Pass	4 ♠	

CONTRACT: 4 ♠.

West leads the ♢ J which is covered with dummy's ♢ K.

(a) Which tricks does East expect to win in defence and in which order does he expect to win them?

(b) A rich kibitzer in a gay mood, sitting behind East, offers to lay 10–1 against the contract. Do you take the bet?

(110)   *Marks*
                                              5

♡ 6 (or 5).

The ◇ Q looks tempting at first sight—but not a moment longer, for East simply cannot be expected to produce two aces. Yet to beat the contract West must somehow put him in so as to ruff another club himself. Is this possible? Perhaps. If West underleads his ♡ A K, declarer may play dummy's ♡ 10 and East could have the ♡ J. Maybe he hasn't, maybe declarer has a doubleton heart and even if he has three, he ought, no doubt, to play dummy's ♡ Q. For all that, West should give him every chance to go wrong. It is by far the best hope he has of defeating the contract.

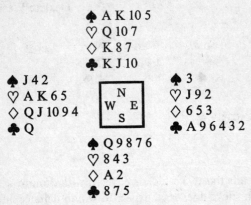

```
                        ♠ A K 10 5
                        ♡ Q 10 7
                        ◇ K 8 7
                        ♣ K J 10
     ♠ J 4 2            ┌─────────┐            ♠ 3
     ♡ A K 6 5          │    N    │            ♡ J 9 2
     ◇ Q J 10 9 4       │ W     E │            ◇ 6 5 3
     ♣ Q               │    S    │            ♣ A 9 6 4 3 2
                        └─────────┘
                        ♠ Q 9 8 7 6
                        ♡ 8 4 3
                        ◇ A 2
                        ♣ 8 7 5
```

ANSWERS

(a) A top trump (the ace or king); the ◇ A; a diamond ruff; the ♣ A.   4

(b) No, the odds aren't good enough.   1

West must have a doubleton diamond. The ◇ J cannot be a singleton, since West opened 1 NT, and with three or more diamonds he would not have led the unsupported jack. Therefore, East should duck, encouraging with the ◇ 10 and leaving West a diamond to play when he comes in with the ♠ A or ♣ K.

For his 1 NT opening (12–14) West must have: ♠ A or K J; ♡ K; ◇ J (played); ♣ A.

Can he have a doubleton K J of spades? No. South would then have eight spades to the ace (or K J) and if so, he would have surely bid 4 ♠, not 3 ♠. So West will have a trump left to ruff the third diamond—providing that East holds up his ace.

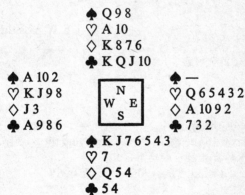

QUESTIONS

(112)

♠ J 10 3
♡ A K J 10 2
◇ Q 2
♣ 9 7 2

```
    N
 W     E
    S
```

♠ A 4 2
♡ Q 9 8 7
◇ 8 4
♣ K 10 8 3

Both sides vulnerable
Dealer: South

South	North
1 ◇	1 ♡
1 NT	3 NT

E/W pass throughout

CONTRACT: 3 NT.

West leads the ♠ 9.
East wins with the ♠ A, declarer playing the ♠ 3 from dummy
and the ♠ Q from his own hand.
Which card should East play at trick two?

QUESTIONS

(113)

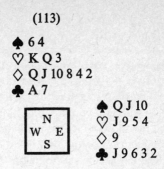

♠ 6 4
♡ K Q 3
◇ Q J 10 8 4 2
♣ A 7

♠ Q J 10
♡ J 9 5 4
◇ 9
♣ J 9 6 3 2

Neither side vulnerable
Dealer: South

South	North
1 NT (12–14)	3 NT

E/W pass throughout

CONTRACT: 3 NT.

West leads the ♠ 7.
Declarer takes East's ♠ 10 with the ♠ K, crosses to dummy with a heart and leads the ◇ Q which holds.
At trick four he leads the ◇ J.
What should East discard?

(112)   *Marks*

♣ 10.   5

There can be no future in spades, for on the lead declarer is marked with the king. He bid diamonds, so that suit, too, looks unattractive. A switch to clubs is clearly indicated, but to which one? The ♣ 3, the fourth highest? That might do if West turned up with two club honours. Meanwhile, the ♣ 10 is likely to be far more effective, helping to catch declarer's jack, as in the diagram below. It will be a good lead, too, if declarer has Q J 6 5 and West holds the A 4.

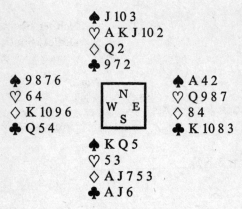

```
                    ♠ J 10 3
                    ♡ A K J 10 2
                    ◇ Q 2
                    ♣ 9 7 2
♠ 9 8 7 6                              ♠ A 4 2
♡ 6 4           ┌───────────┐        ♡ Q 9 8 7
◇ K 10 9 6      │    N      │        ◇ 8 4
♣ Q 5 4         │  W   E    │        ♣ K 10 8 3
                │    S      │
                └───────────┘
                    ♠ K Q 5
                    ♡ 5 3
                    ◇ A J 7 5 3
                    ♣ A J 6
```

ANSWERS

Marks

♠ Q.   10

West is obviously holding up the ♦ A (or K) and he must be thirsting for information. For all he knows, declarer has the ♠ Q, and if so, East must be given the lead at once to play a spade through the closed hand. West is waiting anxiously to see if East·can signal an entry.

East, of course, has no entry, but he can solve West's problem by applying the Rule of Eleven. The lead was the ♠ 7 and 11–7 leaves 4. So the three hands other than West's have between them four cards higher than the seven and East has seen them all—three in his own hand and the fourth, the ♠ K, in declarer's. West, then, can reel off all his spades, though he doesn't know it. To enlighten him, East should throw his ♠ Q, showing that his ♠ 10 at trick one was the lowest of three touching honours.

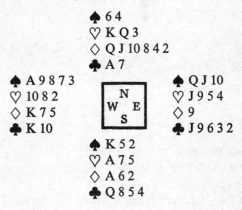

```
            ♠ 6 4
            ♡ K Q 3
            ◇ Q J 10 8 4 2
            ♣ A 7
♠ A 9 8 7 3            ♠ Q J 10
♡ 10 8 2      N       ♡ J 9 5 4
◇ K 7 5    W   E      ◇ 9
♣ K 10        S       ♣ J 9 6 3 2
            ♠ K 5 2
            ♡ A 7 5
            ◇ A 6 2
            ♣ Q 8 5 4
```

QUESTIONS

(114)

♠ K 5
♡ 10 9 7
◇ A K Q 4
♣ J 6 5 3

♠ Q 10 2
♡ A 8 6 5
◇ J 2
♣ Q 7 4 2

```
    N
 W     E
    S
```

Both sides vulnerable
Dealer: South

South	North
Pass	1 ◇
1 ♠	1 NT
2 ♠	

E/W pass throughout

CONTRACT: 2 ♠.

West leads the ♣ 2.

Dummy plays low, East the ♣ 9 and the trick is won with the
♣ A in the closed hand.

At trick two, declarer leads a spade to dummy's king and
another to his jack and West's queen. East follows with the ♠ 4
and ♠ 8.

(a) Which card should West lead when he comes in with the ♠ Q?

(b) Which tricks does he expect to take and in which order does he
    expect to make them?

QUESTIONS

(115)

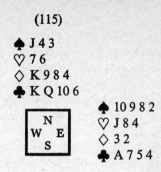

♠ J 4 3
♡ 7 6
◇ K 9 8 4
♣ K Q 10 6

        ♠ 10 9 8 2
        ♡ J 8 4
        ◇ 3 2
        ♣ A 7 5 4

N/S vulnerable
Dealer: South

South	West	North	East
1 ♠	2 ♡	2 ♠	Pass
4 ♠			

CONTRACT: 4 ♠.

West leads the ♡ K.
Which card should East play?

239

ANSWERS

(114)

Marks

(*a*) ♡ 5.   5

(*b*) Two hearts (East's ♡ K Q) ♣ K; ♡ A; ♠ 10.   5

West should be able to place every card that matters.

Declarer must have one more club, the eight, for had East the ♣ 8, he wouldn't have played the ♣ 9. Can South have the ♣ K, too? No. With ♠ A J x x x and ♣ A K, he wouldn't have passed as dealer.

If declarer had two diamonds only he would have discarded his losing club on a diamond before touching trumps. With four diamonds he would have bid 2 ◇, partner's suit, over 1 NT.

With six spades he would have called 3 ♠ or 4 ♠, not 2 ♠.

So declarer is marked with five spades, three diamonds and two clubs, and therefore with three small hearts—small because with the ♡ Q or ♡ K he would be too good to bid as he did.

West now knows that East has the ♡ K Q x and three spades. He followed with the ♠ 8, the second time, so his remaining spade is the nine—and that is the key card.

After cashing two top hearts and the ♣ K, East puts West in to lead the thirteenth heart. East UPPERCUTS, ruffing with the ♠ 9 and so promoting his partner's ♠ 10.

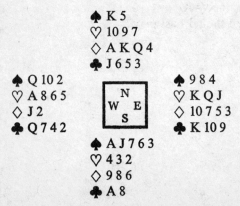

```
              ♠ K 5
              ♡ 10 9 7
              ◇ A K Q 4
              ♣ J 6 5 3
♠ Q 10 2          N          ♠ 9 8 4
♡ A 8 6 5      W     E       ♡ K Q J
◇ J 2             S          ◇ 10 7 5 3
♣ Q 7 4 2                    ♣ K 10 9
              ♠ A J 7 6 3
              ♡ 4 3 2
              ◇ 9 8 6
              ♣ A 8
```

(115)

♡ J.

If declarer can be persuaded that East has a doubleton heart, he may ruff the third heart with dummy's ♠ J, promoting East's ten.

East can tell from the bidding that South must have the ♢ A and that unless defenders develop a trump trick, the contract will not be beaten. But East can also tell—and South can't—that the trumps will break badly. A deceptive high-low heart signal is the best way to exploit this piece of exclusive information.

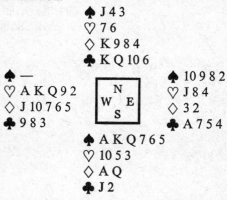

```
                    ♠ J 4 3
                    ♡ 7 6
                    ♢ K 9 8 4
                    ♣ K Q 10 6
    ♠ —                              ♠ 10 9 8 2
    ♡ A K Q 9 2         N            ♡ J 8 4
    ♢ J 10 7 6 5    W       E        ♢ 3 2
    ♣ 9 8 3             S            ♣ A 7 5 4
                    ♠ A K Q 7 6 5
                    ♡ 10 5 3
                    ♢ A Q
                    ♣ J 2
```

QUESTIONS

(116)

♠ 6 3
♡ K 8 3
◇ K Q 7
♣ A Q 10 9 2

```
        N
    W       E
        S
```

♠ A 9 4 2
♡ 4
◇ A J 10 3
♣ K 5 4 3

Neither side vulnerable
Dealer: South

South	West	North	East
Pass	Pass	1 NT	Pass
2 ♡	Pass	Pass	Dble
3 ♡			

CONTRACT: 3 ♡.

West led the ♠ K.

E/W defended well and though South had no loser in trumps, the contract was defeated.

Which five tricks did E/W make and in which order did they make them?

QUESTIONS

(117)

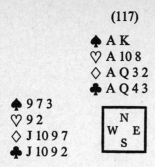

♠ A K
♡ A 10 8
◇ A Q 3 2
♣ A Q 4 3

♠ 9 7 3
♡ 9 2
◇ J 10 9 7
♣ J 10 9 2

Neither side vulnerable
Dealer: South

South	West	North	East
Pass	Pass	2 ♣	2 ♡
Pass	Pass	Dble	Pass
2 ♠	Pass	2 NT	Pass
4 ♠			

CONTRACT: 4 ♠.

West leads the ♡ 9.
Declarer wins with dummy's ♡ A, lays down the ♠ A and ♠ K—East following—and at trick four plays a heart. East wins with the ♡ J and continues with the ♡ K.
Declarer follows.
Which tricks should defenders take and in which order should they take them?

ANSWERS

Marks

♠ A; ♣ K; ♠ Q; ◇ A and ◇ 10.   5

East can see five potential tricks, but the danger is obvious. Unless he sets up two diamond tricks while he still has his ♣ K, declarer will discard any losing diamonds he may have on dummy's clubs. Fortunately, the lead shows that West has a certain entry, the ♠ Q. But there is no time to lose. So East overtakes West's ♠ K to lead the ◇ J. One of dummy's diamond honours is driven out. When East comes in with the ♣ K, he gives West the lead with the ♠ Q to play another diamond through dummy's ◇ K (Q) 7 and all is well.

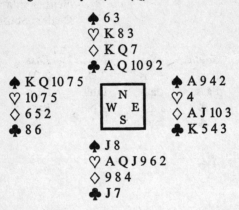

```
                ♠ 6 3
                ♡ K 8 3
                ◇ K Q 7
                ♣ A Q 10 9 2
♠ K Q 10 7 5        ┌─────┐        ♠ A 9 4 2
♡ 10 7 5           │  N  │        ♡ 4
◇ 6 5 2          W │     │ E      ◇ A J 10 3
♣ 8 6              │  S  │        ♣ K 5 4 3
                   └─────┘
                ♠ J 8
                ♡ A Q J 9 6 2
                ◇ 9 8 4
                ♣ J 7
```

ANSWERS

(117)

♠ 9, *ruffing East's* ♡ K, then the kings in both minors.   10

On the bidding, South must have six spades. If he had the king in either minor, which is improbable anyway, he would have eleven tricks on top. So East has both kings and in view of his 2 ♡ bid, South isn't likely to misguess.

If East remains on play with the ♡ K (trick five), he will have to lead another heart (a club or a diamond would be worse). Declarer will ruff and lead out his three remaining trumps. With four cards left, dummy will have ◇ A Q and ♣ A Q, and East ◇ K x and ♣ K x. Declarer will play the ace and queen of one suit, throwing in East and forcing him to play away from his king in the other.

To avert the end-play, West should ruff East's ♡ K and lead one of his jacks through dummy. In itself West's third trump is useless. As a means of seizing the initiative it is invaluable.

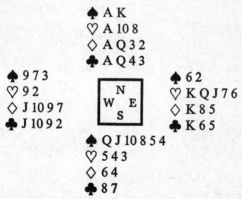

QUESTIONS

(118)

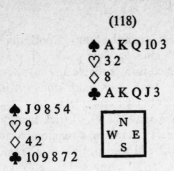

♠ A K Q 10 3
♡ 3 2
◇ 8
♣ A K Q J 3

♠ J 9 8 5 4
♡ 9
◇ 4 2
♣ 10 9 8 7 2

E/W vulnerable
Dealer: South

South	West	North	East
Pass	Pass	1 ♣	1 ♡
2 ◇	Pass	2 ♠	Pass
2 NT	Pass	3 ♠	Pass
3 NT			

CONTRACT: 3 NT.

West leads the ♡ 9.
East goes up with the ♡ K and continues with the ♡ A and ♡ J.
Declarer wins the third trick with the ♡ Q.
What should West discard on the second and third hearts?

QUESTIONS

(119)

♠ 2
♡ K Q 10 9
◇ 10 8 5
♣ K J 10 8 6

♠ 9 7 6 5
♡ J 8 4 2
◇ A K Q
♣ Q 3

Neither side vulnerable
Dealer: North

South	North
—	Pass
1 ♡	3 ♡
4 ♡	

E/W pass throughout

CONTRACT: 4 ♡.

West leads the three top diamonds.
All follow.
At trick four West plays the ♠ 5, East the ♠ J and declarer
the ♠ A.
Declarer leads the ♡ 6.
Which card should West play?

ANSWERS

(118)   *Marks*
                                                      5

One diamond and one spade.

Obviously East must have the ◊ A. Without a certain
entry he would have played low to the first heart, hoping that
partner had another and that communications could be kept
open.

South doesn't know about the bad spade break and it
should be enough for West to keep ♠ J x x x. It had better
be, for if declarer has a hunch and finesses he will make nine
tricks whether West keeps four spades or five.

Observe what happens if West throws both his 'useless'
diamonds to retain the fifth spade. Discovering the position
in the black suits, after two rounds of each, declarer plays out
the clubs. Thrown in with the last club, West must play away
from his ♠ J x x up to dummy's K 10.

While the value of West's fifth spade is purely illusory, the
little diamond is indispensable—as a means of communication.

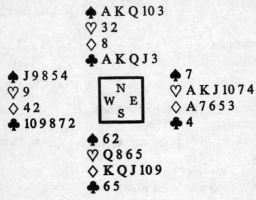

(119)

♡ 8.

5

West has legitimate aspirations to a trump trick, yet declarer can catch the jack—if he knows where it is. To mislead him West should follow with the ♡ 8 suggesting a singleton (or ♡ J 8 bare). Declarer may now play trumps the wrong way, the king, then the queen from dummy, retaining the ace in the closed hand to deal with East's supposed jack.

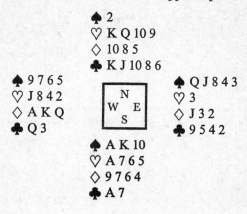

QUESTIONS

(120)

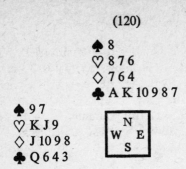

```
              ♠ 8
              ♡ 8 7 6
              ◇ 7 6 4
              ♣ A K 10 9 8 7
♠ 9 7
♡ K J 9              N
◇ J 10 9 8      W         E
♣ Q 6 4 3           S
```

Neither side vulnerable
Dealer: South

South	North
2 ♣	3 ♣
3 ♠	4 ♣
4 ◇	5 ♣
6 ♠	

E/W pass throughout

CONTRACT: 6 ♠.

West leads a trump.

Declarer wins and leads out four more top trumps.

East follows all the way, while West throws a club and two hearts.

At trick six declarer leads the ♡ 3 which falls to West's king, now bare.

Which card should West lead—from: ◇ J 10 9 8; ♣ Q 6 4— to the next trick?

QUESTIONS

(121)

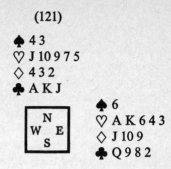

♠ 4 3
♡ J 10 9 7 5
◇ 4 3 2
♣ A K J

♠ 6
♡ A K 6 4 3
◇ J 10 9
♣ Q 9 8 2

E/W vulnerable
Dealer: West

South	West	North	East
—	Pass	Pass	1 ♡
4 ♠			

CONTRACT: 4 ♠.

West leads the ◇ K, the ◇ A and then the ◇ Q.
Declarer ruffs and leads out six trumps.
West follows three times, then he throws two diamonds and the
♣ 4.
Dummy's last four cards are: ♡ J; ♣ A K J.
What should East keep?

Marks
8

A low club.

What is declarer up to? He must have the ♡ A, for other-wise all the remaining hearts could be run against him. Why, then, did he play the ♡ 3? There can be but one answer—to RECTIFY THE COUNT, to concede in good time the inevitable loser.

That is a sure sign that a squeeze is in preparation. South bid diamonds, so the squeeze would threaten either defender if he happened to be long in both minors, as West is here. What can West do about it? He can break up the impending squeeze by leading a club. If declarer has one club only, and it's likely enough, his link with dummy will be cut.

Try playing a diamond instead of a club and see what happens when declarer plays the ♡ A, the squeeze card.

Try another experiment. Take up South's cards and see if you can make 6 ♠ without first conceding a heart. The task is hopeless.

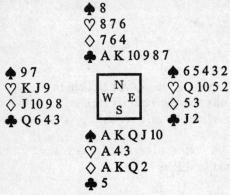

ANSWERS

Marks

♡ 6 and ♣ Q 9 8.

Having seen West, who passed as dealer, produce the
◇ A K Q, declarer will certainly place East with the two top
hearts, and if he bares his ace (or king), he will be thrown in
with it to lead a club into dummy's A K J.

Even if he didn't know who had the ♡ Q, East should take
a chance and throw his top hearts to avoid the end-play. But,
of course, East knows that his partner has the ♡ Q. Had
South the queen, he would have played it long ago, losing to
East's ace. Then he would have crossed to dummy with a
club and led the ♡ J, confidently playing East for the ♡ K.

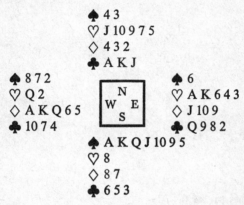

```
              ♠ 4 3
              ♡ J 10 9 7 5
              ◇ 4 3 2
              ♣ A K J
  ♠ 8 7 2                      ♠ 6
  ♡ Q 2          N             ♡ A K 6 4 3
  ◇ A K Q 6 5  W   E           ◇ J 10 9
  ♣ 10 7 4        S            ♣ Q 9 8 2
              ♠ A K Q J 10 9 5
              ♡ 8
              ◇ 8 7
              ♣ 6 5 3
```

(122)

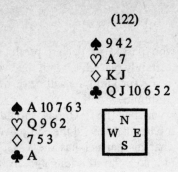

♠ 9 4 2
♡ A 7
◇ K J
♣ Q J 10 6 5 2

♠ A 10 7 6 3
♡ Q 9 6 2
◇ 7 5 3
♣ A

Both sides vulnerable
Dealer: South

South	*North*
1 NT	3 NT
(16–18)	

E/W pass throughout

CONTRACT: 3 NT.

West leads the ♠ 6.
East plays the ♠ J and declarer wins with the ♠ Q.
At trick two a club is played and West is in with the ♣ A.
What should West lead at trick three?

QUESTIONS

(123)

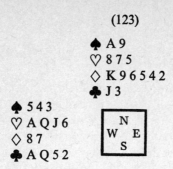

♠ A 9
♡ 8 7 5
◇ K 9 6 5 4 2
♣ J 3

♠ 5 4 3
♡ A Q J 6
◇ 8 7
♣ A Q 5 2

```
N
W   E
S
```

Neither side vulnerable
Dealer: West

South	West	North	East
—	1 NT (12–14)	Pass	Pass
Dble	Pass	Pass	2 ♣
3 ♠	Pass	4 ♠	

CONTRACT: 4 ♠.

West leads the ◇ 8.

Declarer wins with the ◇ A in his hand, leads a diamond to dummy's king and ruffs a third diamond with the ♠ 2.

Which tricks does West hope to win in breaking the contract?

ANSWERS

Marks

♠ A.   5

Crediting South with 16 points, a minimum for his opening, West can see 37 at least round the table. So it's not much
use trying to put East in to lead a spade through the closed
hand, for he can hardly have the ♡ K let alone the ◇ A. Yet
West must act quickly, for as soon as declarer regains the
lead he will reel off a lot of tricks.

The only hope for the defence is that South started with
the ♠ K Q bare, and here West's chances are better, perhaps,
than they look.

By winning the first trick with the ♠ Q declarer advertised
that he had the king, too. One would have expected him to
take the ♠ J with the ♠ K, leaving the position of the ♠ Q
in doubt.

Why did declarer leak so obligingly information about his
♠ K? Was it, by any chance, to put West off from laying
down the ♠ A?

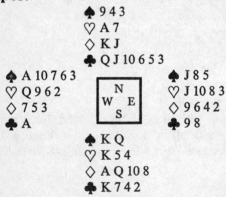

Marks

Four tricks in hearts and clubs, but *no* over-ruff.   8

West mustn't over-ruff the ♠ 2. That is the key to the
defence. Why? Because the ♠ 2 is a highly suspicious card.
Declarer's bidding promises six good spades and he could certainly afford something better than the deuce—unless he
wanted West to over-ruff. Look at the diagram and you will
see why declarer was so anxious to present West with a Greek
gift.

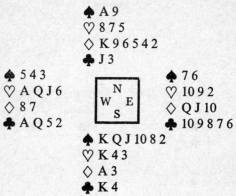

```
              ♠ A 9
              ♡ 8 7 5
              ◇ K 9 6 5 4 2
              ♣ J 3
♠ 5 4 3                      ♠ 7 6
♡ A Q J 6      N             ♡ 10 9 2
◇ 8 7       W     E          ◇ Q J 10
♣ A Q 5 2      S             ♣ 10 9 8 7 6
              ♠ K Q J 10 8 2
              ♡ K 4 3
              ◇ A 3
              ♣ K 4
```

QUESTIONS

(124)

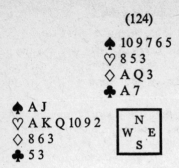

♠ 10 9 7 6 5
♡ 8 5 3
♢ A Q 3
♣ A 7

♠ A J
♡ A K Q 10 9 2
♢ 8 6 3
♣ 5 3

```
  N
W   E
  S
```

Both sides vulnerable
Dealer: North

South	*West*	*North*	*East*
—	—	Pass	Pass
1 ♠	2 ♡	3 ♠	Pass
4 ♠			

CONTRACT: 4 ♠.

West leads the ♡ K, then the ♡ Q.
All follow.
Which card should West play at trick three?

QUESTIONS

(125)

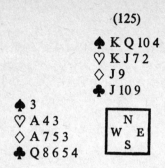

♠ K Q 10 4
♥ K J 7 2
♦ J 9
♣ J 10 9

♠ 3
♥ A 4 3
♦ A 7 5 3
♣ Q 8 6 5 4

N
W E
S

E/W vulnerable
Dealer: North

South	North
—	Pass
1 ♠	3 ♠
6 ♠	

E/W pass throughout

CONTRACT: 6 ♠.

West leads the ♣ 5.

Declarer takes East's ♣ K with the ace and leads two rounds of trumps to which East follows. He then leads a diamond to dummy's jack and another to his ♦ K and West's ♦ A. East follows with the ♦ 2 and ♦ 6.

Which card should West lead when he comes in with the ♦ A?

(124)

Marks
5

♡ 9.

West must be asking himself: 'Where shall I find the fourth trick to break this contract? Even if South has the barest minimum, there's nothing left for poor East. And yet he may have a vital card, the ♠ 8. If I under-lead my hearts, East will have to ruff, and if it's with the eight, declarer will have to over-ruff with the king (or queen) and I shall score two tricks with my A J.'

A point to bear in mind is that, regardless of the distribution, this defence can gain, but cannot cost a trick.

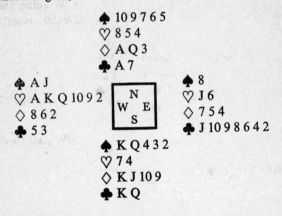

```
                    ♠ 10 9 7 6 5
                    ♡ 8 5 4
                    ◇ A Q 3
                    ♣ A 7
  ♠ A J                             ♠ 8
  ♡ A K Q 10 9 2      N            ♡ J 6
  ◇ 8 6 2          W     E         ◇ 7 5 4
  ♣ 5 3               S            ♣ J 10 9 8 6 4 2
                    ♠ K Q 4 3 2
                    ♡ 7 4
                    ◇ K J 10 9
                    ♣ K Q
```

Marks

♣ Q.

5

West should look to the bidding for an answer to his problem. Lacking controls in two suits, South would have surely sought a little information from his partner. A cue bid of 4 ♣ or a Blackwood 4 NT would have been the normal procedure. His direct jump to 6 ♠ points strongly to a void in hearts.

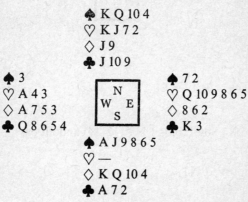

```
              ♠ K Q 10 4
              ♡ K J 7 2
              ◇ J 9
              ♣ J 10 9
  ♠ 3                         ♠ 7 2
  ♡ A 4 3          N          ♡ Q 10 9 8 6 5
  ◇ A 7 5 3     W     E       ◇ 8 6 2
  ♣ Q 8 6 5 4      S          ♣ K 3
              ♠ A J 9 8 6 5
              ♡ —
              ◇ K Q 10 4
              ♣ A 7 2
```

QUESTIONS

(126)

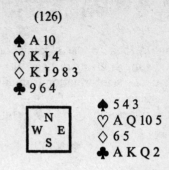

♠ A 10
♡ K J 4
◇ K J 9 8 3
♣ 9 6 4

♠ 5 4 3
♡ A Q 10 5
◇ 6 5
♣ A K Q 2

E/W vulnerable
N/S 60
Dealer: South

South bids 1 NT (12–14) and all pass.

CONTRACT: 1 NT.

West leads the ♡ 9.

Declarer plays dummy's jack and East's queen wins. South follows with the deuce.

What card should East play at trick two?

QUESTIONS

(127)

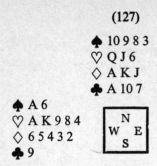

♠ 10 9 8 3
♡ Q J 6
◇ A K J
♣ A 10 7

♠ A 6
♡ A K 9 8 4
◇ 6 5 4 3 2
♣ 9

DUPLICATE PAIRS
Neither side vulnerable
Dealer: North

South	West	North	East
—	—	1 ♣	Pass
1 ♠	Dble	2 ♠	Pass
3 ♣	Pass	4 ♠	

CONTRACT: 4 ♠.

West leads the ♡ K.
East plays the ♡ 10 and declarer the deuce.
Which card should West lead at trick two?

(126)   *Marks*

♣ 2.   5

After a quick look at dummy, East congratulates himself
on his cautious pass. North has enough to raise to 3 NT, but
was lying low, at the score.

Partner can't have a thing and yet, after his lucky opening,
the contract may be broken, if only he can be put in to lead
another heart through dummy. Is it possible? There is just a
chance. West may have the ♣ J—or else the ♣ 10 and declarer, not suspecting the distribution, plays low—as happened when this hand came up in a London club.

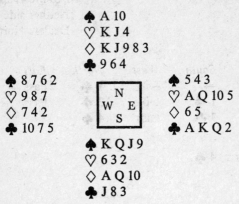

```
                    ♠ A 10
                    ♡ K J 4
                    ◇ K J 9 8 3
                    ♣ 9 6 4
   ♠ 8 7 6 2                          ♠ 5 4 3
   ♡ 9 8 7          N                 ♡ A Q 10 5
   ◇ 7 4 2       W     E              ◇ 6 5
   ♣ 10 7 5         S                 ♣ A K Q 2
                    ♠ K Q J 9
                    ♡ 6 3 2
                    ◇ A Q 10
                    ♣ J 8 3
```

(127)   *Marks*

♣ 9.   5

The contract is doomed anyway, but if West succumbs to temptation and continues hearts to give East a quick ruff, the defence will win the first four tricks—but no more thereafter. And one down is not likely to be a particularly good result.

With a little foresight, West can do better. First he gets rid of his club by leading it at trick two. Then, when he comes in with the ♠ A, he leads the ♡ K and a third heart for East to ruff. Now a club ruff yields the defence a fifth trick.

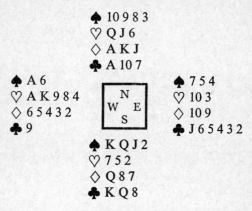

```
              ♠ 10 9 8 3
              ♡ Q J 6
              ◇ A K J
              ♣ A 10 7
♠ A 6                           ♠ 7 5 4
♡ A K 9 8 4      N              ♡ 10 3
◇ 6 5 4 3 2    W   E            ◇ 10 9
♣ 9              S              ♣ J 6 5 4 3 2
              ♠ K Q J 2
              ♡ 7 5 2
              ◇ Q 8 7
              ♣ K Q 8
```

QUESTIONS

(128)

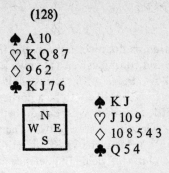

♠ A 10
♡ K Q 8 7
◇ 9 6 2
♣ K J 7 6

♠ K J
♡ J 10 9
◇ 10 8 5 4 3
♣ Q 5 4

N/S vulnerable
Dealer: North

South	North
—	1 ♣
1 ♠	1 NT
3 ♠	4 ♠

E/W pass throughout

CONTRACT: 4 ♠

West leads the ◇ A, then the ◇ K and continues with the ♣ 10. Declarer plays the ♣ J from dummy and takes East's ♣ Q with the ♣ A. He then plays a trump to the ace and another to East's king. West follows suit with the ♠ 3, then the ♠ 4.

Will declarer make his contract if East returns:

(a) A diamond?
(b) A heart?
(c) A club?

QUESTIONS

(129)

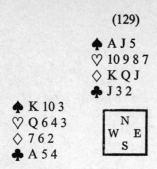

♠ A J 5
♡ 10 9 8 7
◇ K Q J
♣ J 3 2

♠ K 10 3
♡ Q 6 4 3
◇ 7 6 2
♣ A 5 4

N
W E
S

Neither side vulnerable
Dealer: South

South	North
1 NT (12–14)	2 ♣ (Stayman)
2 ◇	3 NT

E/W pass throughout

CONTRACT: 3 NT.

West leads the ♡ 3.
East plays the deuce. Winning with the ♡ J, declarer leads the
♣ 10, the ♣ K and then the ♣ Q.
East follows all the way.
Which card should West lead to trick five when he comes in
with the ♣ A?

ANSWERS

(128)   *Marks*

(*a*) Yes.   4

(*b*) No.   3

(*c*) No.   3

Since West followed in trumps in the natural order, the ♠ 3 before the ♠ 4, he has no more and cannot ruff a diamond.

If West has two trumps, South had seven. His diamonds must be the Q J x and he must also have a second club, for with the ♣ A bare he would have had no reason to play dummy's ♣ J.

That accounts for twelve of declarer's cards. What is the thirteenth? The ♡ A? Impossible. He would have been far too good to bid 3 ♠ on the second round. That applies, also, if in lesser measure, to a void in hearts, but here there is another consideration. With six hearts to the ace and the ◊ A K, West would have doubtless found a bid over 1 ♠. So South must have a heart.

Suppose that East, when he is in with the ♠ K (trick five), returns a diamond. Declarer will win and play out five more trumps. When he leads the last one he will have left one club and one heart, West will have the ♡ A and the ♣ 9 8, while dummy's last three cards will be: ♡ K and ♣ K 7—and West will have to play first.

Note that a club return by East will break up the squeeze by severing declarer's only link with dummy.

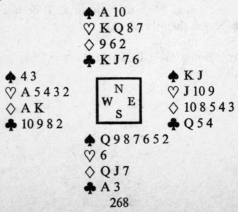

```
                    ♠ A 10
                    ♡ K Q 8 7
                    ◊ 9 6 2
                    ♣ K J 7 6
    ♠ 4 3                        ♠ K J
    ♡ A 5 4 3 2      N           ♡ J 10 9
    ◊ A K          W   E         ◊ 10 8 5 4 3
    ♣ 10 9 8 2       S           ♣ Q 5 4
                    ♠ Q 9 8 7 6 5 2
                    ♡ 6
                    ◊ Q J 7
                    ♣ A 3
```

ANSWERS

Marks

♠ 10.   8

Prospects do not seem too bright, and yet East may have
the ♠ 9 in which case the contract can be beaten—if spades
are attacked at once.

Declarer has shown 5 points in clubs (♣ K Q) and he must
have 8 in hearts since East couldn't find the ♡ A or ♡ K.
That is 13 points. With ◇ A or the ♠ Q as well, South would
have too much for a weak 1 NT. Therefore West has both. He
must also have four (or five) spades in view of South's 2 ◇
response to 2 ♣, denying a four-card major.

If the ♠ 10 isn't covered it will hold the trick. Should declarer cover with dummy's ♠ J, the ♠ Q will win and a low
spade to the ♣ K will drive out the ♠ A. East will still have
a certain entry in the ◇ A.

Note that East's spades cannot be brought in if West leads
the ♠ K. Dummy's ♠ A will win and West will not get in
again to play through the ♠ J 5.

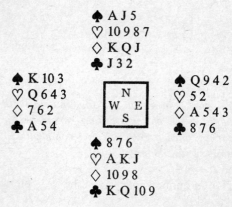

♠ A J 5
♡ 10 9 8 7
◇ K Q J
♣ J 3 2

♠ K 10 3   ♠ Q 9 4 2
♡ Q 6 4 3   N   ♡ 5 2
◇ 7 6 2   W   E   ◇ A 5 4 3
♣ A 5 4   S   ♣ 8 7 6

♠ 8 7 6
♡ A K J
◇ 10 9 8
♣ K Q 10 9

QUESTIONS

(130)

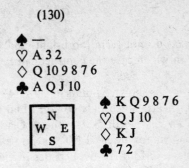

♠ —
♡ A 3 2
◇ Q 10 9 8 7 6
♣ A Q J 10

♠ K Q 9 8 7 6
♡ Q J 10
◇ K J
♣ 7 2

N/S vulnerable
Dealer: South

South	West	North	East
1 ♡	Pass	3 ◇	4 ♠
Pass	5 ♠	Pass	Pass
6 ♡			

CONTRACT: 6 ♡.

This hand was played in a teams of four match. With a certain trump trick and the ◇ K J poised over the diamond bidder, East had no temptation to sacrifice in 6 ♠. He felt confident that he could defeat 6 ♡—until he saw dummy.

West opened the ♠ J.

Declarer ruffed in dummy and played the ♡ A on which West threw a small spade.

At trick three declarer led dummy's ◇ 6.

The contract went one down.

Which were East-West's two winners?

QUESTIONS

(131)

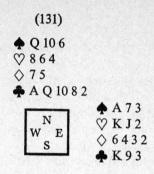

♠ Q 10 6
♡ 8 6 4
◇ 7 5
♣ A Q 10 8 2

	N	
W		E
	S	

♠ A 7 3
♡ K J 2
◇ 6 4 3 2
♣ K 9 3

N/S vulnerable
Dealer: South

South	*North*
1 NT	3 NT
(16–18)	

E/W pass throughout

CONTRACT: 3 NT.

West leads the ♠ 5.
Declarer plays the ♠ 6 from dummy and East the ♠ 7.
(a) If declarer wins with the ♠ K, which card should East lead when he comes in with the ♣ K?
(b) Which card should East lead, when he is in with the ♣ K, if declarer wins the first trick with the ♠ J?

271

(130)

$\Diamond$ J and a trump trick.

At trick three East made the spectacular play of the $\Diamond$ K on dummy's six.

He knew that declarer couldn't have the ♣ K, for that would have given him twelve tricks. But he knew, too, and declarer didn't, that the club finesse would succeed and that if he had a losing diamond, he would have no difficulty in parking it on a club.

To give declarer a chance to go wrong, East created the illusion of a 'marked' finesse against the $\Diamond$ J in place of an even money chance in clubs.

East could well afford to 'throw away' his $\Diamond$ K for in the ordinary way he couldn't expect to take a trick with it.

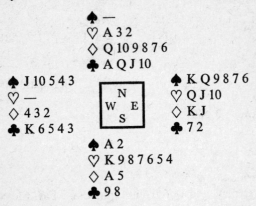

(131)

(*a*) ♡ K.   5
(*b*) ♠ A.   3

The correct defence hinges on DISCOVERY. East should apply the RULE OF ELEVEN. West led the 5, and 11−5=6. East can see five of the six cards higher than the five, leaving one for declarer. By playing the ♠ 7 he finds out which it is. If it's the king, there can be no future in spades, for dummy has a second stopper. Now the only hope is to find partner with something like ♡ A 10 x x.

If, however, declarer wins the first trick with any spade other than the king—the J or 9 or 8—West plays the ♠ A and the ♠ 3, in the knowledge that partner can take the rest of the tricks in the suit.

Declarer's hand could be:

　　♠ J 4　　♡ A Q 9 2　　◇ A K Q　　♣ J 7 6 4
　　　　　　　　　　　　or
　　♠ K 4　　♡ Q 9 2　　◇ A K Q J　　♣ J 7 6 4

QUESTIONS

(132)

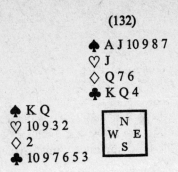

♠ A J 10 9 8 7
♡ J
◇ Q 7 6
♣ K Q 4

♠ K Q
♡ 10 9 3 2
◇ 2
♣ 10 9 7 6 5 3

N
W E
S

N/S vulnerable
Dealer: South

South	West	North	East
1 ♡	Pass	1 ♠	2 ◇
4 ♡			

CONTRACT: 4 ♡.

West leads his singleton ◇ 2.
Declarer plays low from dummy and East, winning with the
◇ J, continues with the ◇ K.
Declarer follows with the ◇ 3, then the ◇ 9.
Which should be West's first discard (trick two)?

QUESTIONS

(133)

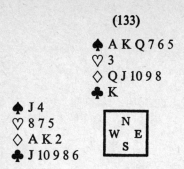

♠ A K Q 7 6 5
♡ 3
♢ Q J 10 9 8
♣ K

♠ J 4
♡ 8 7 5
♢ A K 2
♣ J 10 9 8 6

```
    N
W       E
    S
```

Both sides vulnerable
Dealer: West

South	North
—	1 ♠
2 ♣	2 ♢
2 NT	3 ♠
3 NT	

E/W pass throughout

CONTRACT: 3 NT.

West opens the ♣ J to dummy's king.

East follows with the deuce.

At trick two declarer leads dummy's ♢ Q. East plays the ♢ 3 and declarer the ♢ 5.

(*a*) Which card should West play?

(*b*) Which card should West play when he comes in with the ♢ K?

(132)

♠ K.

On the ◇ A he will discard the ♣ Q. Thereafter nothing can prevent him from making a spade ruff for the setting trick.

Note that declarer must have a third diamond. East won the first trick with the ◇ J and the ◇ 10 is still missing.

```
                    ♠ A J 10 9 8 7
                    ♡ J
                    ◇ Q 7 6
                    ♣ K Q 4
♠ K Q                  ┌───────┐              ♠ 6 5 4 3 2
♡ 10 9 3 2             │   N   │              ♡ 4
◇ 2                    │ W   E │              ◇ A K J 8 5 4
♣ 10 9 7 6 5 3         │   S   │              ♣ 2
                       └───────┘
                    ♠ —
                    ♡ A K Q 8 7 6 5
                    ◇ 10 9 3
                    ♣ A J 8
```

(133)

(*a*) ♢ K.

3

(*b*) ♠ J.

2

East's ♢ 3 must be his lowest since West has the deuce himself. So East has three diamonds—with a doubleton he would have started a high-low signal—and West must, therefore, win. Note that if he doesn't, declarer will only need the heart finesse to make his contract.

If declarer has two spades the contract is probably unbeatable. West must hope that he has a singleton, which is likely enough on the bidding, and he leads his ♠ J to cut communications between declarer and dummy. The effect of this can be seen from the diagram below. Declarer can no longer develop nine tricks.

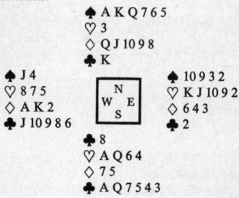

$$\begin{array}{c} \spadesuit \text{ A K Q 7 6 5} \\ \heartsuit \text{ 3} \\ \diamondsuit \text{ Q J 10 9 8} \\ \clubsuit \text{ K} \end{array}$$

♠ J 4   ♠ 10 9 3 2
♡ 8 7 5   ♡ K J 10 9 2
♢ A K 2   ♢ 6 4 3
♣ J 10 9 8 6 ♣ 2

N
W E
S

♣ 8
♡ A Q 6 4
♢ 7 5
♣ A Q 7 5 4 3

QUESTIONS

(134)

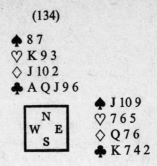

♠ 8 7
♡ K 9 3
◇ J 10 2
♣ A Q J 9 6

♠ J 10 9
♡ 7 6 5
◇ Q 7 6
♣ K 7 4 2

E/W vulnerable
Dealer: South

South	West	North	East
1 ♡	1 ♠	2 ♣	Pass
4 ♡	Pass	5 ♡	Pass
6 ♡			

CONTRACT: 6 ♡.

West leads the ♠ K.
Declarer wins with the ♠ A and runs the ♣ 10 to East's ♣ K.
What should East play at trick three?

QUESTIONS

(135)

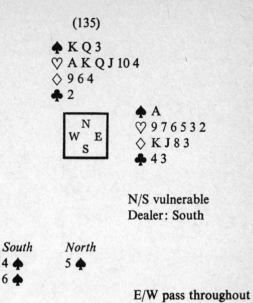

♠ K Q 3
♡ A K Q J 10 4
♢ 9 6 4
♣ 2

♠ A
♡ 9 7 6 5 3 2
♢ K J 8 3
♣ 4 3

N/S vulnerable
Dealer: South

South	North
4 ♠	5 ♠
6 ♠	

E/W pass throughout

CONTRACT: 6 ♠.

West led ♢ 2.

East went up with the ♢ K. Winning with the ace, declarer led a trump to East's ace.

East felt sure that declarer had a loser somewhere. But what was it? A diamond or a club?

What should East have done to make certain of finding the right answer?

(134)

Marks

A diamond.　　　　　　　　　　　　　　　　　　10

Why didn't declarer draw trumps before touching clubs? There can only be one reason: he didn't want to give West a chance to signal. Other things being equal, East would have returned a spade. Therefore, the feared signal, making other things unequal, would have been a high diamond.

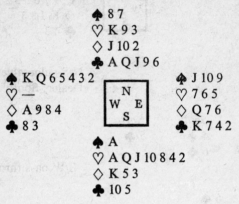

```
                  ♠ 8 7
                  ♡ K 9 3
                  ◇ J 10 2
                  ♣ A Q J 9 6
  ♠ K Q 6 5 4 3 2         ♠ J 10 9
  ♡ —           N         ♡ 7 6 5
  ◇ A 9 8 4  W     E      ◇ Q 7 6
  ♣ 8 3           S       ♣ K 7 4 2
                  ♠ A
                  ♡ A Q J 10 8 4 2
                  ◇ K 5 3
                  ♣ 10 5
```

ANSWERS

Marks

East should have played the ◇ J at trick one. 8

West might have led the ◇ 2 from the ◇ Q, but he was hardly likely to underlead an ace against a slam. There could be no objection, therefore, to 'finessing against partner' by playing the ◇ J. And it would have brought to light a vital clue. Had declarer taken the ◇ J with the ◇ A, East would have known that his other loser was a diamond. South had a diamond, of course, since West would not have led the deuce from a five-card suit. If, however, declarer won the first trick with the ◇ Q—as would have been the case here—East would have led a club at trick three.

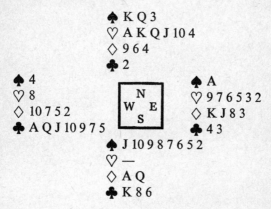

```
              ♠ K Q 3
              ♡ A K Q J 10 4
              ◇ 9 6 4
              ♣ 2
 ♠ 4                          ♠ A
 ♡ 8              N           ♡ 9 7 6 5 3 2
 ◇ 10 7 5 2   W     E         ◇ K J 8 3
 ♣ A Q J 10 9 7 5   S         ♣ 4 3
              ♠ J 10 9 8 7 6 5 2
              ♡ —
              ◇ A Q
              ♣ K 8 6
```

QUESTIONS

(136)

♠ A K Q J
♡ A J
◇ K Q 4 2
♣ 8 3 2

♠ 10 9 8
♡ K Q
◇ J 10 9 8
♣ A K J 5

N
W   E
S

Both sides vulnerable
Dealer: North

South	North
—	1 ◇
1 NT	3 NT

E/W pass throughout

CONTRACT: 3 NT.

West leads the ♣ K, then the ♣ A.
East encourages with the ♣ 7, then the ♣ 4. Declarer follows
with the ♣ 10 and ♣ Q.
As soon as declarer gains the lead he plays off dummy's spades.
What card should West discard on the fourth spade?

QUESTIONS

(137)

♠ 7 6 5 3
♡ J 9 5
◇ A Q 5
♣ A K 2

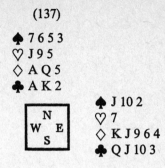

♠ J 10 2
♡ 7
◇ K J 9 6 4
♣ Q J 10 3

Neither side vulnerable
Dealer: West

South	*North*
—	1 NT (12–14)
4 ♡	

E/W pass throughout

CONTRACT: 4 ♡.

West leads out the three top spades.
Declarer ruffs the third spade and leads the ♡ A, the ♡ K and
a low heart to dummy's jack, West following all the way.
Next, declarer plays dummy's fourth spade (trick seven).
Which should be East's last six cards?

(136)   *Marks*
                                              10
♣ J.

Yes, this means that West should have switched to some other suit at trick three. Even if he has never heard of squeezes he should look ahead and think of the future. Clubs will yield four tricks only and if he cashes them all, what will he throw on the fourth spade? He will be inexorably squeezed in the red suits for South must surely have the ◇ A.

If he switches at trick three—any suit will do, though the ♡ K is the natural card to play—he will have the ♣ J available for a discard. He retains the ♣ 5, of course, to give the lead to East whose fourth club will be the setting trick.

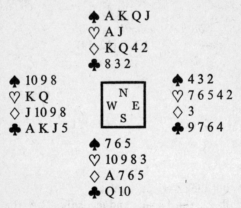

```
                    ♠ A K Q J
                    ♡ A J
                    ◇ K Q 4 2
                    ♣ 8 3 2
 ♠ 10 9 8                          ♠ 4 3 2
 ♡ K Q              N              ♡ 7 6 5 4 2
 ◇ J 10 9 8      W     E           ◇ 3
 ♣ A K J 5          S              ♣ 9 7 6 4
                    ♠ 7 6 5
                    ♡ 10 9 8 3
                    ◇ A 7 6 5
                    ♣ Q 10
```

ANSWERS

(137)

$\diamond$ K J 9 and $\clubsuit$ Q J 3.

Having drawn trumps and eliminated spades, declarer will play three rounds of clubs, and unless East gets out of the way, he will be end-played—thrown in with a club and forced to lead a diamond into dummy's A Q. He should, therefore, throw a club honour at some stage, retaining the $\clubsuit$ 3 as an *exit card*.

Should East keep all his clubs leaving himself with $\diamond$ K J (or 9), declarer will play ace, then small, setting up the $\diamond$ Q for his tenth trick.

Why shouldn't he take the diamond finesse instead? Because he has heard West pass as dealer and he has seen him produce already the $\spadesuit$ A K Q. He is not likely to have the $\diamond$ K, too.

$\spadesuit$ 7 6 5 3
$\heartsuit$ J 9 5
$\diamond$ A Q 5
$\clubsuit$ A K 2

$\spadesuit$ A K Q 9
$\heartsuit$ 6 4 2
$\diamond$ 10 8 7
$\clubsuit$ 9 7 6

N
W E
S

$\spadesuit$ J 10 2
$\heartsuit$ 7
$\diamond$ K J 9 6 4
$\clubsuit$ Q J 10 3

$\spadesuit$ 8 4
$\heartsuit$ A K Q 10 8 3
$\diamond$ 3 2
$\clubsuit$ 8 5 4

QUESTIONS

(138)

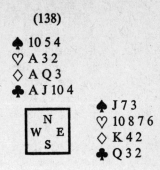

♠ 10 5 4
♡ A 3 2
◇ A Q 3
♣ A J 10 4

♠ J 7 3
♡ 10 8 7 6
◇ K 4 2
♣ Q 3 2

Neither side vulnerable
Dealer: South

South	North
1 NT (12–14)	3 NT

E/W pass throughout

CONTRACT: 3 NT.

West led the ♡ K, ♡ Q and ♡ J.

Declarer, who followed all the way, ducked twice. Going up with dummy's ♡ A the third time, he crossed to his hand with a spade to the ♠ A and ran the ◇ J.

East defended well and the contract was beaten.

Which tricks did defenders take and in which order did they take them?

QUESTIONS

(139)

```
                    ♠ K 8 5
                    ♡ A 9 7
                    ◇ 9 7 6 5
                    ♣ 10 7 6
   ♠ 4 3 2        ┌─────────┐
   ♡ Q J 10 5     │    N    │
   ◇ K 4          │ W     E │
   ♣ A K 8 4      │    S    │
                  └─────────┘
```

Both sides vulnerable
Dealer: West

South	West	North	East
—	1 ♣	Pass	Pass
Dble	Pass	1 ◇	Pass
2 ♠	Pass	3 ♠	Pass
4 ♠			

CONTRACT: 4 ♠.

West leads the ♣ K, the ♣ A and the ♣ 4 to East's ♣ J.
Declarer ruffs the third club and leads out five trumps,
discarding two diamonds from dummy. East follows once, with
the ♠ J. His four subsequent discards are: ♡ 2; ◇ 2; ◇ 3; and
♣ Q.
Which should be West's last five cards?

ANSWERS

(138)

Marks
10

♢ K, ♣ Q and ♡ 10.

When East came in with the ♢ K he returned a spade—or another diamond. He did *not* cash the last heart. Thinking, as East intended him to do, that West had the thirteenth heart, declarer took the club finesse into East's hand. *Then* East scored his ♡ 10.

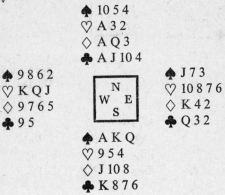

```
              ♠ 10 5 4
              ♡ A 3 2
              ♢ A Q 3
              ♣ A J 10 4
♠ 9 8 6 2          ┌─────┐          ♠ J 7 3
♡ K Q J           │  N  │           ♡ 10 8 7 6
♢ 9 7 6 5       W │     │ E         ♢ K 4 2
♣ 9 5             │  S  │           ♣ Q 3 2
                   └─────┘
              ♠ A K Q
              ♡ 9 5 4
              ♢ J 10 8
              ♣ K 8 7 6
```

(139)

Marks

♡ Q J 10 5 and ◇ K.

8

Declarer must know a lot about the hand by now. East, who couldn't keep 1 ♣ open, has turned up already with the ♠ J and the ♣ Q J. He cannot have the ◇ K, too, so whatever he does, declarer won't finesse.

Whether declarer's last five cards are ♡ K x ◇ A Q x or ♡ K x x ◇ A Q, he will be tempted to throw West in with a heart, forcing him to play away from the ◇ K.

Anticipating this end-play, West should bare his ◇ K, preferably before discarding his last club. He will follow in hearts with the ♡ 10 and ♡ J, pretending to have started with three hearts only, the Q J 10.

Note that East must co-operate. If he loses interest, takes his eye off the ball and discards two of his wretched hearts, he will give the show away by not following to hearts on the second round.

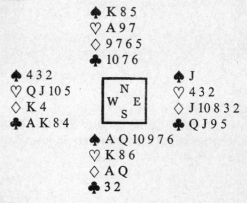

♠ K 8 5
♡ A 9 7
◇ 9 7 6 5
♣ 10 7 6

♠ 4 3 2
♡ Q J 10 5
◇ K 4
♣ A K 8 4

♠ J
♡ 4 3 2
◇ J 10 8 3 2
♣ Q J 9 5

♠ A Q 10 9 7 6
♡ K 8 6
◇ A Q
♣ 3 2

QUESTIONS

(140)

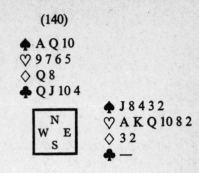

♠ A Q 10
♡ 9 7 6 5
◇ Q 8
♣ Q J 10 4

♠ J 8 4 3 2
♡ A K Q 10 8 2
◇ 3 2
♣ —

Both sides vulnerable
Dealer: East

South	*West*	*North*	*East*
—	—	—	1 ♡
3 ◇	Pass	5 ◇	

CONTRACT: 5 ◇.

West leads the ♡ 3.
East wins with the ♡ Q and declarer follows with the ♡ 4.
On which further tricks can defenders count with certainty and
in which order will they make them?

(141)

♠ A K Q J
♡ 2
♢ A Q J 8
♣ A K 10 4

```
      ┌─────┐      ♠ 10 4 3 2
      │  N  │      ♡ A J 4 3
      │W   E│      ♢ 9 7
      │  S  │      ♣ 9 7 3
      └─────┘
```

N/S vulnerable
Dealer: East

South	West	North	East
—	—	—	Pass
Pass	1 ♡	2 ♡	3 ♡
3 ♠	Pass	6 ♠	

CONTRACT: 6 ♠.

West leads the ♡ K.
Which card should East play?

(140)   *Marks*

♡ 2, ruffed by West; a club, ruffed by East.   5

West's ♡ 3 must be a singleton. Only the ♡ J is missing and West wouldn't have led the ♡ 3 from J 3. So declarer has one more heart. East must not cash his ♡ K (or A), however, or it will be the last trick for his side. He must underlead his tops, compelling partner to ruff—and to lead a club for East to ruff.

West may know nothing of signals, of Lavinthal or of McKenney, but he will ask himself: What's going on? Why is East putting me forcibly on play? He can't possibly want a spade. So he must want a club. Here goes. . . .

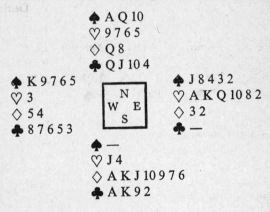

```
                    ♠ A Q 10
                    ♡ 9 7 6 5
                    ◇ Q 8
                    ♣ Q J 10 4
  ♠ K 9 7 6 5                      ♠ J 8 4 3 2
  ♡ 3              ┌─────────┐     ♡ A K Q 10 8 2
  ◇ 5 4            │   N     │     ◇ 3 2
  ♣ 8 7 6 5 3      │ W   E   │     ♣ —
                   │   S     │
                   └─────────┘
                    ♠ —
                    ♡ J 4
                    ◇ A K J 10 9 7 6
                    ♣ A K 9 2
```

ANSWERS

♡ A.   *Marks*
                                                                              5

East should overtake and return another heart, forcing declarer to ruff in dummy and so ensuring a trick for his ♠ 10.

If East plays the ♡ J, West might read it as a SUIT PRE-FERENCE SIGNAL and switch to a diamond. Whether West would be right or wrong to do so, is immaterial. Since East can beat the contract on his own, he should not give West the chance to go wrong.

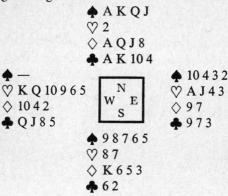

```
                    ♠ A K Q J
                    ♡ 2
                    ◇ A Q J 8
                    ♣ A K 10 4
    ♠ —                           ♠ 10 4 3 2
    ♡ K Q 10 9 6 5     N          ♡ A J 4 3
    ◇ 10 4 2        W     E       ◇ 9 7
    ♣ Q J 8 5          S          ♣ 9 7 3
                    ♠ 9 8 7 6 5
                    ♡ 8 7
                    ◇ K 6 5 3
                    ♣ 6 2
```

(142)

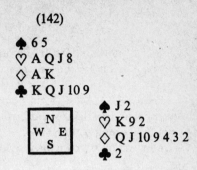

♠ 6 5
♡ A Q J 8
◇ A K
♣ K Q J 10 9

              ♠ J 2
              ♡ K 9 2
              ◇ Q J 10 9 4 3 2
              ♣ 2

MATCH POINTED PAIRS
Neither side vulnerable
Dealer: West

West	North	East	South
Pass	1 ♣	3 ◇	Pass
3 ♠	Dble	Pass	4 ♡

CONTRACT: 4 ♡.

West leads the three top spades.
Declarer ruffs the third spade with dummy's ♡ J.
Which card must East find in West's hand to beat the contract?

QUESTIONS

(143)

♠ K Q J 10 2
♡ Q J 7
◇ 8 6
♣ A Q J

N	♠ A 7 5
W E	♡ 3 2
S	◇ A Q J 10 4 2
	♣ 7 6

Neither side vulnerable
Dealer: South

South	West	North	East
Pass	Pass	1 ♠	2 ◇
2 ♡	Pass	3 ♡	Pass
4 ♡			

CONTRACT: 4 ♡.

West leads the ◇ 9.
East wins with the ◇ A and South follows with the ◇ 7.
What should East play at trick two?

ANSWERS

♡ 10.

There is no other hope. Had West the ♣ A, as well as a spade suit headed by the three tops, he wouldn't have passed as dealer.

East, of course, mustn't think of over-ruffing. If he does, he will earn a bottom every time and get it—some of the time, when West turns up with the ♡ 10. He should throw his ♣ 2 and later take his ♡ K, and also the ♡ 9, the setting trick.

East has one other chance. Declarer may try to come to his hand with the ♣ A to take the trump finesse, and if so, East will ruff. This would be poor play by declarer who should know that West can hardly have the ♡ K, as well as his good long spades. But declarers do not always play perfectly and this is something defenders should never fail to bear in mind.

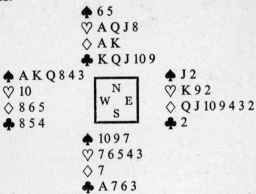

```
                    ♠ 6 5
                    ♡ A Q J 8
                    ◇ A K
                    ♣ K Q J 10 9
 ♠ A K Q 8 4 3    ┌─────┐    ♠ J 2
 ♡ 10             │  N  │    ♡ K 9 2
 ◇ 8 6 5        W │     │ E  ◇ Q J 10 9 4 3 2
 ♣ 8 5 4          │  S  │    ♣ 2
                  └─────┘
                    ♠ 10 9 7
                    ♡ 7 6 5 4 3
                    ◇ 7
                    ♣ A 7 6 3
```

ANSWERS

♠ 5.

Marks

5

East can see two tricks only for the defence, his two aces. But there is hope. South, who passed as dealer, is marked with the ◇ K, so West is quite likely to have a trump trick, the third for his side. Is there any chance of a fourth? Only if West can ruff something. It can't be a club, but he may have a doubleton spade. Then the contract can be beaten, providing that East retains his ♠ A as an entry to play the third spade which West will ruff.

Note that West cannot have a singleton spade. With four spades South would have raised North's major instead of bidding his own.

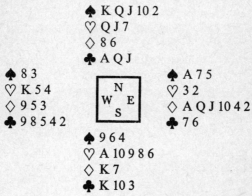

```
              ♠ K Q J 10 2
              ♡ Q J 7
              ◇ 8 6
              ♣ A Q J
  ♠ 8 3         ┌─────────┐      ♠ A 7 5
  ♡ K 5 4       │    N    │      ♡ 3 2
  ◇ 9 5 3       │ W     E │      ◇ A Q J 10 4 2
  ♣ 9 8 5 4 2   │    S    │      ♣ 7 6
                └─────────┘
              ♠ 9 6 4
              ♡ A 10 9 8 6
              ◇ K 7
              ♣ K 10 3
```

QUESTIONS

(144)

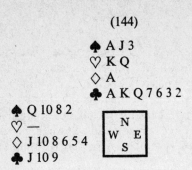

♠ A J 3
♡ K Q
♢ A
♣ A K Q 7 6 3 2

♠ Q 10 8 2
♡ —
♢ J 10 8 6 5 4
♣ J 10 9

```
  N
W   E
  S
```

Both sides vulnerable
Dealer: South

South	North
1 ♡	3 ♣
3 ♡	4 NT
5 ♢	5 NT
6 ♡	7 ♡

E/W pass throughout

CONTRACT: 7 ♡.

West leads the ♢ J to dummy's ace.

Declarer plays the ♡ K, then the ♣ A and the deuce, which he ruffs.

At trick five he leads the ♠ 7.

(a) Which card should West play?

(b) Which trick can defenders hope to win?

QUESTIONS

(145)

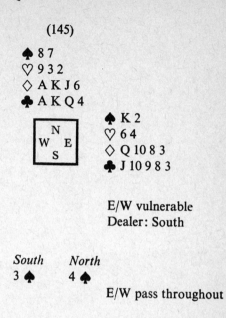

♠ 8 7
♡ 9 3 2
◇ A K J 6
♣ A K Q 4

♠ K 2
♡ 6 4
◇ Q 10 8 3
♣ J 10 9 8 3

E/W vulnerable
Dealer: South

South	North
3 ♠	4 ♠

E/W pass throughout

CONTRACT: 4 ♠.

West leads the ♡ K, then the ♡ A.
Declarer follows with the ♡ J and ♡ Q.
At trick three West leads the ♡ 10.
Which card should East play?

(144)   *Marks*

(a) ♠ Q.   5
(b) ♡ J.   5

Why did declarer ruff a club instead of drawing trumps in the ordinary way? That is the crucial question and West's void in hearts points to the right answer.

Declarer is obviously trying to shorten his trumps. Why? Presumably because East has an unfinessible jack—J x x x— and declarer is trying to catch it. To do so, he must first establish trump parity with East, then lead from dummy. That requires four entries—one for each club ruff and one more to get to dummy for the killing lead through East.

After playing the ♡ K and discovering the bad trump break, declarer was one entry short and hoped to find it in the ♠ J, if West had the ♠ Q.

Can West stop him? Yes, if South's ♠ K is a doubleton. West most hope that it is and go up with the ♠ Q. He has everything to gain and nothing to lose.

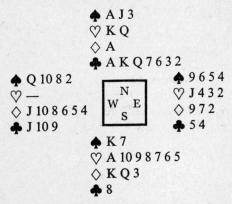

            ♠ A J 3
            ♡ K Q
            ♢ A
            ♣ A K Q 7 6 3 2

♠ Q 10 8 2   ♠ 9 6 5 4
♡ —   ♡ J 4 3 2
♢ J 10 8 6 5 4   ♢ 9 7 2
♣ J 10 9   ♣ 5 4

            ♠ K 7
            ♡ A 10 9 8 7 6 5
            ♢ K Q 3
            ♣ 8

ANSWERS

Marks

♠ K.   5

Declarer can have no losers in the side-suits and the only
hope for the defence is to win two trump tricks. By using the
♠ K for an 'uppercut' East may promote a trump trick for
his partner, and it may be the setting trick, if West's trump
holding is Q 10 (as in the diagram below) or possibly J 9 x.

Whatever the position, playing the ♠ K cannot cost a trick.

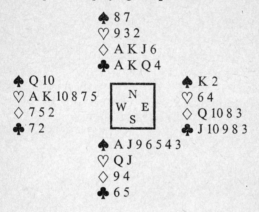

```
                    ♠ 8 7
                    ♡ 9 3 2
                    ◇ A K J 6
                    ♣ A K Q 4
  ♠ Q 10          ┌─────────┐          ♠ K 2
  ♡ A K 10 8 7 5  │    N    │          ♡ 6 4
  ◇ 7 5 2         │ W     E │          ◇ Q 10 8 3
  ♣ 7 2           │    S    │          ♣ J 10 9 8 3
                  └─────────┘
                    ♠ A J 9 6 5 4 3
                    ♡ Q J
                    ◇ 9 4
                    ♣ 6 5
```

QUESTIONS

(146)

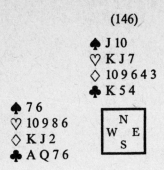

♠ J 10
♡ K J 7
◇ 10 9 6 4 3
♣ K 5 4

♠ 7 6
♡ 10 9 8 6
◇ K J 2
♣ A Q 7 6

Neither side vulnerable
Dealer: South

South	North
1 ♠	1 NT
3 ♡	3 NT
4 ♡	

E/W pass throughout

CONTRACT: 4 ♡.

West leads the ♣ A.
East follows with the three and declarer with the deuce.
Which card should West lead at trick two?

QUESTIONS

(147)

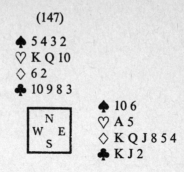

♠ 5 4 3 2
♡ K Q 10
♢ 6 2
♣ 10 9 8 3

♠ 10 6
♡ A 5
♢ K Q J 8 5 4
♣ K J 2

Neither side vulnerable
Dealer: South

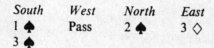

South	West	North	East
1 ♠	Pass	2 ♠	3 ♢
3 ♠			

CONTRACT: 3 ♠.

West leads the ♢ 7.

Declarer takes East's ♢ J with the ♢ A and leads a heart to dummy's ♡ Q.

If the contract is defeated, which tricks will East-West make and in what order will they make them?

(146)   *Marks*

$\diamond$ K.   10

Take five marks for the $\diamond$ 2.

On the bidding, South cannot have more than three cards in the minors and he mustn't be given the chance to throw a losing diamond on the ♣ K. But even if East turns up with the $\diamond$ A, this will only yield the defence three tricks and West can see that should declarer need a finesse in spades, he will bring it off. How, then can a fourth trick be conjured up?

West should try a little hocus-pocus. At trick two, he leads the $\diamond$ K, then the $\diamond$ 2, proclaiming a doubleton. Coming in with the $\diamond$ A, East will play a third diamond. Fearing an over-ruff and knowing nothing of the bad trump break, declarer may well ruff with the $\heartsuit$ Q, promoting a trump trick for West.

Should East turn up unexpectedly with the $\heartsuit$ Q, the contract will fail anyway, but the $\diamond$ K will still be a good shot.

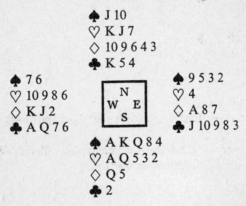

              ♠ J 10
              $\heartsuit$ K J 7
              $\diamond$ 10 9 6 4 3
              ♣ K 5 4

♠ 7 6   ♠ 9 5 3 2
$\heartsuit$ 10 9 8 6   N $\heartsuit$ 4
$\diamond$ K J 2   W E $\diamond$ A 8 7
♣ A Q 7 6   S   ♣ J 10 9 8 3

              ♠ A K Q 8 4
              $\heartsuit$ A Q 5 3 2
              $\diamond$ Q 5
              ♣ 2

ANSWERS

(147)

Marks

♠ K; ◇ K; ♡ A; diamond ruff; heart ruff.   8

The clue to the best defence lies in declarer's play at trick two. Evidently he is intent on leading trumps from dummy. If so, West must have a trump trick, and a quick entry. He will return a diamond and ruff a diamond. Defenders will need one more trick. Can it be conjured up? Yes, if East holds up the ♡ A at trick two. Then, before leading the third diamond for West to ruff, he will cash his ♡ A and ruff West's heart return.

Wouldn't East achieve the same result by going up at once with the ♡ A and returning the ♡ 5? Unlikely. Declarer would be alerted and he would probably lead out his ♠ A. giving up the chance of a trump finesse in favour of some safer play. As the cards are, he would, in fact, make ten tricks.

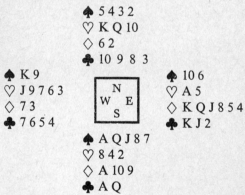

```
                ♠ 5 4 3 2
                ♡ K Q 10
                ◇ 6 2
                ♣ 10 9 8 3
 ♠ K 9                        ♠ 10 6
 ♡ J 9 7 6 3      N           ♡ A 5
 ◇ 7 3         W     E        ◇ K Q J 8 5 4
 ♣ 7 6 5 4        S           ♣ K J 2
                ♠ A Q J 8 7
                ♡ 8 4 2
                ◇ A 10 9
                ♣ A Q
```

(148)

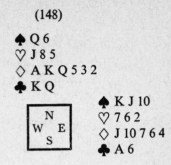

♠ Q 6
♡ J 8 5
◇ A K Q 5 3 2
♣ K Q

♠ K J 10
♡ 7 6 2
◇ J 10 7 6 4
♣ A 6

Neither side vulnerable
Dealer: North

South	North
—	1 ◇
2 ♣	3 ◇
3 NT	

E/W pass throughout

CONTRACT: 3 NT.

West leads the ♡ K.

Declarer wins with the ♡ A and plays a club. West follows with the deuce.

(a) Which card should East play?

(b) Which card should East play when he comes in with the ♣ A?

QUESTIONS

(149)

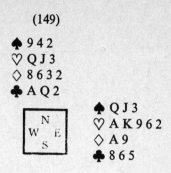

♠ 9 4 2
♡ Q J 3
◇ 8 6 3 2
♣ A Q 2

♠ Q J 3
♡ A K 9 6 2
◇ A 9
♣ 8 6 5

Neither side vulnerable
Dealer: East

South	West	North	East
—	—	—	1 ♡
1 ♠	Pass	2 ♠	Pass
3 ♠			

CONTRACT: 3 ♠.

West leads the ♡ 5.

East wins with the ♡ K and continues with the ♡ A on which West plays the ♡ 4.

Declarer follows with the ♡ 8 and the ♡ 10.

Which card should East lead at trick three?

ANSWERS

Marks

(*a*) ♣ A.

1

(*b*) ♠ K.

7

The purpose of both plays is to prevent declarer from enjoying his clubs.

Going up with the ♣ A at once causes the suit to be blocked in dummy. The ♠ K coming next kills declarer's only possible entry to the clubs—before he can unblock them

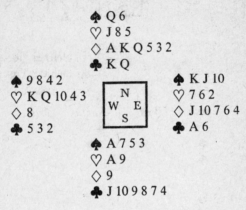

```
                    ♠ Q 6
                    ♡ J 8 5
                    ◇ A K Q 5 3 2
                    ♣ K Q
   ♠ 9 8 4 2                      ♠ K J 10
   ♡ K Q 10 4 3        N          ♡ 7 6 2
   ◇ 8              W     E        ◇ J 10 7 6 4
   ♣ 5 3 2            S           ♣ A 6
                    ♠ A 7 5 3
                    ♡ A 9
                    ◇ 9
                    ♣ J 10 9 8 7 4
```

ANSWERS

Marks

♡ 2.   10

Declarer is obviously false-carding. From ♡ 7 5 4 West
wouldn't have led the ♡ 5, so declarer has the missing ♡ 7
and West will ruff the third heart. What would East like him
to return? A diamond to his ace? That would be distinctly
embarrassing, for if he then led a fourth heart and West
failed to produce a trump higher than dummy's nine, it
would give away the trump position. And if East didn't play
another heart, it would look suspicious. Either way, East's
trump holding would be compromised.

The best way out is for East to lead the ♡ 2, a deceptive
SUIT PREFERENCE SIGNAL, asking for a club. Declarer will
doubtless heave a sigh of relief, lay down the ♠ A—and go
one down.

East needn't worry about the ◇ A. It will always come
into its own—unlike the trump trick, which may easily run
away.

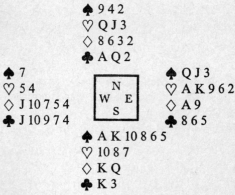

```
              ♠ 9 4 2
              ♡ Q J 3
              ◇ 8 6 3 2
              ♣ A Q 2
 ♠ 7                        ♠ Q J 3
 ♡ 5 4          N           ♡ A K 9 6 2
 ◇ J 10 7 5 4  W   E        ◇ A 9
 ♣ J 10 9 7 4      S        ♣ 8 6 5
              ♠ A K 10 8 6 5
              ♡ 10 8 7
              ◇ K Q
              ♣ K 3
```

QUESTIONS

(150)

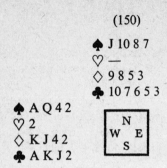

♠ J 10 8 7
♡ —
◇ 9 8 5 3
♣ 10 7 6 5 3

♠ A Q 4 2
♡ 2
◇ K J 4 2
♣ A K J 2

```
    N
 W     E
    S
```

Neither side vulnerable
Dealer: South

South	*West*	*North*	*East*
3 ♡	Dble*	Pass	Pass
Pass			

CONTRACT: 3 ♡ Doubled.

West leads the ♣ K, then the ♣ A.
Declarer follows to the king, ruffs the ace and leads a spade to West's queen.
What card should West lead to trick four?

---

* West's double is for a take-out, but East, obviously with a suitable trump holding, converts it into a penalty double.

(150)   *Marks*

◇ 2.   10

When declarer is marked on the bidding with a long, porous trump suit and little else, defenders should strive to make quickly all their tricks in the side-suits, compelling declarer to lead trumps himself. The switch to a diamond can hardly cost a trick, for it isn't likely that South opened 3 ♡ with the ◇ A Q.

Look at the diagram below and follow the course of events if:

(*a*) declarer has to lead trumps himself;

(*b*) if defenders 'force' him at every opportunity.

As an instructive exercise let defenders take their six winners first, before allowing declarer to ruff anything. Then watch the dénouement. Declarer must lead trumps himself and wins, all told—three tricks!

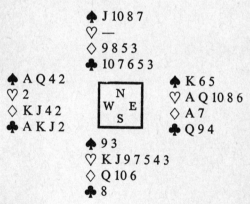

```
              ♠ J 10 8 7
              ♡ —
              ◇ 9 8 5 3
              ♣ 10 7 6 5 3
♠ A Q 4 2        N        ♠ K 6 5
♡ 2           W     E     ♡ A Q 10 8 6
◇ K J 4 2        S        ◇ A 7
♣ A K J 2                 ♣ Q 9 4
              ♠ 9 3
              ♡ K J 9 7 5 4 3
              ◇ Q 10 6
              ♣ 8
```